She cleared he  r?"

The subtle lift of his _____ her, then he hissed s_____ between his teeth an_____ turned to face her. Dark brown hair like his son's, except shaggy and unkempt, framed a face chiseled in stone. His jawbones were high, his face square, his eyes the color of a sunset, brown and orange and gold, rich with color but...dead.

That was the only word to describe the emptiness she saw there.

He removed his Stetson, then walked toward her and held out a work-roughened hand that looked strong enough to break rocks. Everything about the man, from his muscular build, his towering height, his broad shoulders and those muscular thighs, screamed of masculinity.

And a raw sexuality that made her heart begin to flutter.

But anger also simmered beneath the surface of his calm, anger and something lethal, like a bloodthirsty need for revenge.

Jordan tried to ignore the fear that rippled through her. Miles McGregor was a dangerous man.

RITA HERRON

COWBOY COP

HARLEQUIN®
entertain, enrich, inspire™

Recycling programs
for this product may
not exist in your area.

ISBN-13: 978-0-373-69657-4

COWBOY COP

Copyright © 2012 by Rita B. Herron

ABOUT THE AUTHOR

Award-winning author Rita Herron wrote her first book when she was twelve, but didn't think real people grew up to be writers. Now she writes so she doesn't have to get a *real* job. A former kindergarten teacher and workshop leader, she traded her storytelling to kids for writing romance, and now she writes romantic comedies and romantic suspense. She lives in Georgia with her own romance hero and three kids. She loves to hear from readers, so please write her at P.O. Box 921225, Norcross, GA 30092-1225, or visit her website, www.ritaherron.com.

Books by Rita Herron

HARLEQUIN INTRIGUE

*Nighthawk Island
‡‡Guardian Angel Investigations
†Guardian Angel Investigations: Lost and Found
**Bucking Bronc Lodge

CAST OF CHARACTERS

Detective Miles McGregor—Miles will do anything to protect his son and make sure the man responsible for the boy's mother's death pays.

Jordan Keys—Guilt-stricken over her younger brother's death, she's determined to help Timmy. But she can't fall for the boy's father, a handsome Texas cowboy, because he'll leave her like dust in the wind when the case is solved.

Timmy McGregor—The only witness to his mother's murder, but he has no memory of that night....

Marie Younger—Timmy's mother died at the hands of the Slasher. But was she as innocent as she seemed?

Robert Dugan—This smooth-talking businessman was convicted of being the Slasher, but he swears he was set up. Does he want revenge because he was wrongly accused or because Miles pointed out what a monster he is?

Renee Balwinger—She gave Robert Dugan an alibi for the murder of Timmy's mother—but is she lying to protect the man, who also happens to be her lover?

Janet Bridges—Dugan was in love with her, but now she's missing. Is she helping him, or running from him herself?

CeeCee Dugan—Dugan's mother: is she really alive?

Paul Belsa—He was Marie's lover. Could he have killed her instead of Dugan?

Pruitt Ables—What does he have to do with Dugan and the Slasher crimes?

Prologue

The verdict was in.

Perspiration beaded on Detective Miles McGregor's neck. He hoped to hell it was guilty. Robert Dugan deserved to die.

He had killed four women so far, brutal stabbings that had left his victims raw and exposed to the elements, suffering as they bled out, alone and frightened.

The coldhearted bastard.

Marie's face flashed in his mind, a reminder that his son's mother could have been a victim just like these other women.

Remorse hit him for the way their relationship had soured over time. They'd had a brief affair when he was in between cases a few years ago, and she'd gotten pregnant. He'd offered to marry her, but she hadn't wanted it. She said he was married to the job.

That was true. But during this case he'd worried about her. Not because he was in love with her, but he did care, dammit. And his son needed them to be on the same page. To get along.

He'd make it up to her for not being around the past few months. He'd be the man she wanted. The one she deserved.

The father his little boy, Timmy, needed.

He took a deep breath, splashed cold water on his face, then grabbed a paper towel and dried his beard-stubbled face. One look into the mirror and he cursed.

Damn, he looked like hell.

He hadn't slept since this case had started, since he'd seen that first victim's body. He'd thought catching the maniac would help him rest, but still the images haunted him.

Only seeing Dugan rot in jail would ease the pain.

He tossed the paper towel into the trash, strode from the men's room toward the courtroom, then slipped inside and took a seat on the bench behind the prosecutor. He'd testified, and now he wanted to watch the look on Dugan's face when he was convicted and sentenced to death row.

At least he hoped to hell he was convicted. DNA evidence had been iffy, and Dugan had managed to make sure he'd left no witnesses behind, so circumstantial evidence, a partial fingerprint, the profile from the Behavioral Crime Unit and Miles's testimony had made the case.

He wiped his sweaty hands on his pants. It might not be enough.

A low murmur of voices rippled through the courtroom as the door opened, and the jurors filed in, heads bowed, faces pinched and drawn. Twelve people who held the future of one man in their hands.

A future that, if he was released, would cost more women their lives.

Miles had no doubt in his mind about that.

The bailiff cleared his throat. "All rise for the Honorable Judge Fenton."

Everyone stood while the judge entered, then Dugan strode in, his slender face etched with worry in spite of the cool facade he tried to paint as he took his seat.

The judge pounded the gavel, then asked for the verdict, and the jury foreman stood and handed the bailiff the envelope. The man who'd led the jury was a hard-assed construction worker who Miles had liked on sight because he could tell the man had been raised right, to respect women and see through the fake charms of men like Dugan.

A real polished smooth talker who had undoubtedly seduced his way into close proximity to his victims and made them feel safe—until he'd slit their throats.

The soft rustle of clothing and shaky breaths reverberated through the room as the judge opened the envelope and perused its contents. Without batting an eye, he handed the envelope back to the bailiff, who passed it to the foreman.

"Mr. Dugan, please stand for the reading of the verdict," Judge Fenton said.

Miles studied Dugan as he buttoned his suit jacket, then Dugan shot him a smug smile and squared his shoulders.

Judge Fenton gestured toward the foreman and he nodded.

"On the first count of murder, we find Robert Dugan guilty."

Collective sighs of relief filled the room, then heads nodded as the same verdict was handed down for the other three murder charges.

Miles's heart pounded as they polled the jury and a unanimous count was confirmed.

Dugan's breathing faltered slightly, the only sign he was affected by the verdict, then the judge announced that the sentencing would be delivered in three days. Dugan's lawyer, a female who looked as if she too had fallen for Dugan's fake charms, patted his shoulder, mumbling, no doubt, about filing an appeal.

Then the police stepped forward to escort Dugan back to his cell. The crowd dispersed, hushed voices murmuring about whether or not they agreed with the trial's outcome, and Miles shook the prosecutor's hand then stepped into the hallway.

Cameras flashed, reporters swarmed. Dugan's attorney tried to shield him, but her client seemed to like the attention.

In fact, he looked over at Miles and a slow sadistic smile creased his face. Then he mouthed the words *You'll pay.*

Miles's heart pounded, even as he knew that he was safe for now.

But if Dugan was ever released, he'd have to watch his back.

Dugan turned and waved at the crowd, pausing to insist to the press that he was an innocent man. That he'd been framed.

Bile rose in Miles's throat, but he ordered himself not to react. Instead, he stepped outside into the muggy Texas air.

Heat suffused him in a cloud of steam rising from the pavement, and the fact that he hadn't slept for days intensified his fatigue.

He'd vowed to make it up to his son and Marie for leaving them for days on end without so much as checking in, for missing Timmy's birthday and Christmases and the rodeo at the BBL, for being exactly what Marie said he was: married to the job.

He'd start now. This Christmas he would be there to play Santa for his boy.

He headed toward his Jeep but his cell phone chirped—his friend from the Bucking Bronc Lodge and fellow detective Mason Blackpaw, who'd worked the Slasher case with him.

A bad feeling pinched his gut.

Was Blackpaw calling to congratulate him on the verdict or for another reason?

He punched the connect button. "You heard the verdict, Mason?"

"Yeah. But we have a problem." Blackpaw hissed a sound of disgust that confirmed Miles's earlier premonition.

"What?"

"There was another murder."

Miles gritted his teeth at the words he didn't want to hear. "Where? Who?"

"Another woman, name's June Kelly."

"And?"

"It's not good, McGregor. Her throat was slit just like the other four."

Miles dropped his head into his hands and cursed. *Dammit, no.*

The M.O. was the same as the murders Dugan had just been convicted of.

Which meant Dugan was either innocent, he had a partner or there was a copycat killer.

No...he was sure Dugan was guilty.

But hell, this was bad—even if Dugan was in jail, a killer was still out there hunting....

Chapter One

Three months later

"Dugan is out."

Miles's fingers tightened around his cell phone as he wheeled his SUV around and headed toward the station. "What?"

His superior, Lieutenant Hammond, didn't sound happy. "Based on the Kelly woman's murder and some technicality with the chain of evidence when they'd searched the man's place, Dugan's lawyer got his conviction overturned."

The past few weeks of tracking down clues and false leads day and night taunted him. He released a string of expletives.

Hammond cleared his throat. "If we'd found evidence connecting Dugan to a partner, maybe things would have gone differently, but…"

Hammond let the sentence trail off, but Miles silently finished for him. If he and Mason had found such evidence, Dugan would still be in a cell. And the world would be a safer place.

But they'd failed.

The day Dugan's verdict was read flashed back. Dugan's threat resounded in his head—*you'll pay*.

"Now that he's back on the streets—"

"I know. He's going to kill again," Miles said. *And he's probably coming after me.*

His cell phone chirped, and he glanced at the caller ID. Marie's number.

Damn, she was probably on his case for working again last night and missing dinner with Timmy. He'd thought he might have found a lead on the copycat, but instead he'd only chased his own tail.

The phone chirped again.

You'll pay.

Panic suddenly seized him, cutting off his breath. Dammit…what if payback meant coming after his family?

"I have to go, Hammond." Sweat beaded on his neck as he connected the call. "Hello?"

Husky breathing filled the line, then a scream pierced the receiver.

He clenched the steering wheel with a white-knuckled grip. He had to clear his throat to speak. "Marie?" *God, tell me you're there….*

But the sudden silence sent a chill up his spine.

"Marie, Timmy?"

More breathing, this time followed by a husky laugh that sounded sinister, threatening…evil.

Dear God, no…

Dugan was at Marie's house.

He pressed the accelerator, his heart hammering as he sped around traffic and called for backup. The dispatch officer agreed to send a patrol car right away.

A convertible nearly cut him off, and Miles slammed on his horn, nearly skimming a truck as he roared around it. Brush and shrubs sailed past, the wheels grinding on gravel as he hugged the side of the country road.

Images of the dead women from Dugan's crime scenes flashed in his head, and his stomach churned. No, please, no…Dugan could not be at Marie's house. He couldn't kill Marie…not like the other women.

And Timmy…his son was home today with her.

The bright Texas sun nearly blinded him as he swerved into the small neighborhood where Marie had bought a house. Christmas decorations glittered, lights twinkled from the neighboring houses, the entryways screaming with festive holiday spirit.

Somehow they seemed macabre in the early-morning light.

He shifted gears, brakes squealing as he rounded a curve and sped down the street. He scanned the neighboring yards, the road, the trees beyond the house, searching for Dugan.

But everything seemed still. Quiet. A homey little neighborhood to raise a family in.

Except he had heard that scream.

His chest squeezed for air, and he slammed on the brakes and skidded up the drive. He threw the Jeep into Park, and held his weapon at the ready as he raced up to the front door.

Cop instincts kicked in, and he scanned the outside of the house and yard again, but nothing looked amiss. He glanced through the front window, but the den looked normal…toys on the floor, magazines on the table, TV running with cartoons.

Only the Christmas tree had been tipped over, ornaments scattered across the floor.

He reached for the doorknob, and the door swung open. His breath lodged in his throat, panic knotting his insides. No sounds of holiday music or Timmy chattering.

Gripping his weapon tighter, he inched inside, senses honed for signs of an intruder.

Slowly, he made his way through the den to the kitchen. The Advent calendar glared at him, mocking him with a reminder that Christmas was only a few days away.

There was a half-empty coffee cup on the counter and an

overturned cereal bowl on the table. Milk dripped onto the floor.

Timmy…God…

Terror seized him.

A creaking sound suddenly splintered the air, and he swung around, braced to shoot but he saw nothing. Then another sound came from above, water running…the shower? No, the tub…overflowing…

He clenched his jaw, then inched toward the staircase, slowly climbing it and listening for an intruder, for Marie, for his son.

Any sign of life.

A quick glance into Timmy's room and it appeared empty. Bed unmade. Toy airplane on the floor. Legos scattered. Stuffed dinosaur on his pillow.

Where was his son?

His hand trembled as he bypassed the room and edged toward the bedroom where Marie slept. One look inside, and his heart stopped.

The lamp was broken on the floor. Pillows tossed on the carpet. The corner chair overturned. Glass shards from the mirror were scattered on the vanity.

A sea of red flashed in front of him. Blood…it soaked the sheets and led a trail into the bathroom.

His stomach revolted, but he forced himself to scan the corners of the room before slowly entering the bathroom. Blood streaked the floor and led toward the claw-foot tub.

A groan settled deep in his gut.

Marie. Her eyes stood wide-open in death. Blood dripped down her neck and bare chest. Her arms dangled lifelessly over the tub edge, one leg askew.

For a moment, he choked. Couldn't make himself move. He'd seen dozens of dead bodies before but none so personal… none that he cared about.

Emotions crowded his throat and chest, and he gripped the wall to steady himself. He had to. Had to get control. Slide that wall back into place so he could do his job.

Every second counted.

Fighting nausea, he slowly walked toward her and felt for a pulse. Although he knew before he touched her that it was too late.

Dugan had done this. Had gotten his payback by killing his son's mother.

That creaking sound suddenly echoed again. He froze, hand clenching his gun, then spun around.

Nothing. Except the evidence of Dugan's brutal crime.

Where was Timmy?

For a fraction of a second he closed his eyes on a prayer. The sound echoed again…

The attic.

Heart hammering double-time, he headed toward Timmy's room. The door to the space had been built inside his closet. Timmy had called it his secret room.

Had Dugan found it?

Hope warred with terror as he inched inside the closet and pushed at the door. It was closed, but he had insisted the lock be removed for fear Timmy might lock himself inside and be trapped.

Now he wished he'd left that damn lock on so his son could have locked Dugan out.

Darkness shrouded the cavernous space as he climbed the steps. He tried to move soundlessly, but the wood floor squeaked. As he reached the top step, a sliver of sunlight wormed its way through the small attic window, allowing him to sweep the interior.

It appeared empty, but he had heard *something*.

"Timmy," he whispered. "Son, are you here?"

Praying he was safe, Miles examined the room. Timmy's toy airplanes and horses, his train set…

Another squeak, and he jerked his head around. An antique wardrobe sat in the corner, one Marie had used to store old quilts. He held his breath as he approached it, then eased open the door.

Relief mingled with pain when he saw his little boy hunched inside, his knees drawn to his chest, his arms wrapped around them. He had buried his head against his legs, silent sobs racking his body.

"Timmy, it's okay, it's Dad." Anguish clogged his throat as he gently lifted his son's face. Blood dotted Timmy's T-shirt and hands, and tears streaked his splotched skin, a streak of blood on his left cheek.

But it was the blank look in his eyes that sent a wave of cold terror through Miles.

Timmy might be alive, but he was in shock.

He stooped down to Timmy's level and dragged him into his arms, but his son felt limp, as if the life had drained from him just as it had his mother.

Three weeks later

JORDAN KEYS WATCHED the busload of new campers arrive at the Bucking Bronc Lodge, her heart in her throat. The troubled kids ranged from ages five to sixteen.

Her brother had fit in that category. But he was gone now.

Because she hadn't been able to help him.

She fisted her hands, silently vowing to do better here. She'd read about the BBL and how hard the cowboys and staff worked to turn these kids' lives around, and she wanted to be a part of it.

If she saved just one kid, it might assuage some of her guilt over her brother's death.

A chilly January wind swirled dried scrub brush across the dirt and echoed through the trees. She waved to Kim Woodstock, another one of the counselors and Brandon Woodstock's wife, as she greeted the bus, then Jordan bypassed them and headed straight into the main lodge to meet with Miles McGregor and his five-year-old son, Timmy.

Apparently Miles also volunteered at the BBL, but this time he'd come because he needed solace and time to heal from a recent loss.

So did his little boy, who they believed had witnessed his mother's murder.

A thread of anxiety knotted her shoulders as she let herself in the lodge. The empty spot where the Christmas tree had stood made the entryway seem dismal, but truth be told, she was glad it was gone. The holidays always resurrected memories of Christmases past, both good and bad memories that tormented her with what-ifs.

Shoving the thoughts to the back of her mind, she grabbed a cup of coffee and made her way back to the wing Brody Bloodworth had recently added to serve as a counseling and teen center.

The moment she stepped into the room, she sensed pain emanating through it. Like a living, breathing entity smothering the air.

Little Timmy, a dark-haired boy who looked scrawny and way too pale, sat in the corner against the wall, his knees drawn up, his arms locked tightly around them as if he might crumble if he released his grip. The poor child didn't even look up as she entered, simply sat staring through glazed eyes at some spot on the floor as if he was lost.

For a moment, she couldn't breathe. What if she failed this little guy, too? What if he needed more than she could give?

Inhaling to stifle her nerves, she pasted on a smile, then glanced at the cowboy standing by the window watching the horses gallop across the pasture. His back was to her, his wide shoulders rigid, his hands clenching the window edge so tightly she could see the veins bulging in his broad, tanned hands.

She cleared her throat. "Mr. McGregor?"

The subtle lift of his shoulders indicated he'd heard her, then he hissed something low and indiscernible between his teeth and slowly turned to face her. Dark brown hair like his son's, except his was shaggy and unkempt, framed a face chiseled in stone. His jawbones were high, his face square, his eyes the color of a sunset, brown and orange and gold, rich with color, but…dead.

That was the only word to describe the emptiness she saw there.

He removed his Stetson, then walked toward her and held out a work-roughened hand that looked strong enough to break rocks. Everything about the man, from his muscular build, his towering height, his broad shoulders and those muscular thighs, screamed of masculinity.

And a raw sexuality that made her heart begin to flutter.

But anger also simmered beneath the surface of his calm, anger and something lethal, like a bloodthirsty need for revenge.

She didn't know all the details about his relationship to Timmy's mother, but she understood that anger. She also knew where it led…to nothing good.

"I'm Jordan Keys," she said, finally finding her voice. "Nice to meet you."

"There's nothing nice right now," he said in a gruff voice.

Jordan stiffened slightly. Obviously he was in pain, but did that mean he didn't want her help? A lot of men thought counseling was bogus, for sissies…beneath them.

"Maybe not, but you're here now, and I see you brought

your little boy." She gestured toward Timmy, who still remained oblivious to her appearance. "So let's talk."

He worked his mouth from side to side as if he wanted to say something, but he finally gave a nod. "Brody filled you in?"

"Briefly. But I'd like to hear the details from you."

"Of course. We've seen doctors—"

"Not in front of Timmy," Jordan said, cutting him off. "Let me talk to him for a minute, then we can step outside and discuss the situation."

His mouth tightened into a grim line, but he nodded again. This man didn't like to be ordered around, didn't like to be out of control.

And he had no control right now.

Which was obviously killing him.

She understood that feeling as well.

She slowly walked over and knelt beside the child. "Timmy, my name is Miss Jordan. I'm glad you came to the BBL. We have horses here and other kids to play with and lots of fun things planned."

His eye twitched, but he didn't reply or look at her.

"Why don't you sit at the table? There are markers and paper. Maybe you can draw about Christmas."

Again, he didn't move.

Miles touched his son's shoulder. "Why don't you draw the bike Santa brought you?"

Again, no response.

"Come on, sport." Miles took his arm and led the boy to the table. Timmy slumped down in the chair, but he didn't pick up the markers. He simply stared at the blank paper as if he was too weighted down to move.

"I need to talk to your daddy for a minute," Jordan said, giving his arm a soft pat. "We'll be outside that door if you need us, all right?"

His eyes twitched sideways toward her this time. Frightened.

She rubbed his shoulder gently. "I promise. We're not going anywhere but right outside the room." She gestured toward a glass partition. "See that glass? We'll be in there so if you need us, just call or tap on the glass and we'll come back."

He didn't respond, just tucked his knees up and began to rock back and forth. His bony little body was wound so tight that Jordan felt the tension thrumming through him.

"If you want to draw, that's fine," she said again, using a quiet voice. "If not, you can look out that window and watch the pretty horses running around."

The fact that he didn't turn to look at them worried her. But she simply smiled, then ushered his father into the hallway and into the other room.

When she closed the door, Miles immediately angled his head to watch his son through the partition. Jordan's chest squeezed.

Miles McGregor was one of the biggest, toughest-looking men she'd ever met. He was not only a cowboy, but Brody had told her he was a cop who chased down the dregs of society.

Miles was also hurting inside and felt powerless to help his son. That made them kindred spirits.

"Tell me what happened," Jordan said gently.

He slanted her a condescending look. "I thought you said Brody filled you in."

Jordan simply folded her arms. "Yes, but I want to hear it from you. Everything from the day Timmy's mother died to how and where you found Timmy to what the doctors said."

A muscle jumped in his chiseled jaw. "You can read the police report." He yanked an envelope from inside his denim jacket pocket. The movement revealed the weapon he had holstered to his side. "Here's the doctor's report, too."

Jordan forced a calm into her voice. "I will read it, but it's important I hear what you have to say."

"Why? All I need for you to do is to get Timmy to look at this picture." He yanked another envelope from his jacket, pulled out a photograph and slapped it on the table. "If he can identify this man as his mother's killer, then I can put him back in jail where he belongs."

Jordan gritted her teeth. "So Timmy witnessed the murder?"

Miles gave a clipped nod, the pain so intense in his eyes that it nearly robbed her breath. "I believe so, but he hasn't spoken since that day. That's why I need you to get him to talk."

Jordan glanced through the window at Timmy, her heart aching for the boy. "I understand your impatience," she said. "But Timmy has undergone a terrible shock. It may take him time to open up."

Miles glared at her. "I don't have *time*."

Jordan's anger rose. "Then you'd better damn well find it, because the important thing here is that your son heal."

A muscle ticked in his jaw, his eyes flaring with rage. "The important thing is keeping Timmy safe. This man Robert Dugan is a cold-blooded killer. He threatened me in court, he slit Timmy's mother's throat, and if he knows Timmy is a witness, he'll probably come back to kill him."

TIMMY ROCKED HIMSELF back and forth in the chair. He thought the lady said something to him. Something about horses. But he couldn't make out her words. It was too noisy in his head. Voices…things crashing…the screaming.

And he couldn't see any horses.

All he saw was the red.

Red blotches…black blotches…more red…more black…

Someone else was in the room with him, too. His daddy… at least he thought it was his daddy…

No, he was mad at him. He hadn't come home…

His eyes blurred and then it was dark. So dark everything went black.

Like night all the time. Scary night.

Scary night when the monsters came...

He buried his head in his arms and rocked harder. Pushed at his ears to make the noises be quiet.

He didn't want to see the monsters. They were bad. They were going to get him.

He had to run....

But he couldn't run...he couldn't move. Couldn't do nothing to stop the noises and the dark from coming...

Or the red from splattering the walls...

Or his mommy's cries...

Chapter Two

Miles had never wanted to be anything but a lawman. Not since he was young and Sheriff Silas Weatherby had saved his butt from jail and taken him in as his own.

Miles's old man had used him to help carry out his own crimes. Cattle rustling—not murder like Robert Dugan—but it was illegal and every crime, no matter how small, hurt *somebody.*

Still, Silas had a code of ethics, which meant that he tried to save kids when even their own families had taught them to lie, cheat and steal.

Which was the main reason Miles had chosen to contribute to the BBL. He figured it was payback time.

Yes, Silas had taught Miles right from wrong and given him a chance to become a man and protect others.

Only that job had gotten Timmy's mother killed.

He fisted his hands, sweat beading on his lip as he tried to control the rage burning through him. His son was drowning in a world of hurt because Miles had chosen to do the right thing.

Worse, he was hurting because he'd witnessed a crime that nobody, much less a five-year-old, should have to see.

Miles's gut churned as he stared at the swirls of black and red Timmy had savagely drawn on the pad of paper. Not signs of a happy Christmas or the new bike Santa had brought.

No, dark swirls of colors that Timmy hadn't even seemed to realize he was drawing.

Swirls of colors that it didn't take a rocket scientist—or a shrink—to decipher because that sea of black and red represented the darkness and the blood that his son had seen.

Timmy's mother's blood.

Had he watched Dugan viciously slash her throat?

For just a moment, those images became his own, and Miles's legs nearly buckled as guilt and pain suffused him. If only he'd gone to get Timmy that night and brought him back in the morning like Marie asked, he could have saved her.

Damn Dugan—just like the other murders, he'd left no evidence. And somehow he'd managed to fabricate an alibi for the time of Marie's death.

It had to be a lie.

Even though Blackpaw had suggested that Marie might have had a lover or boyfriend who had killed her and copied Dugan's M.O. to throw off the cops, he couldn't believe it.

Dugan had promised payback and he'd gotten it.

"Mr. McGregor—Miles—" Jordan said. "I understand that you're angry—"

"Wouldn't you be?" Miles's temper exploded, and he whirled on her, needing to vent his frustration, no matter who took the brunt. "Just look at my son. He's traumatized and motherless yet his mother's killer is walking around free. Hell, he's probably bragging about it as he plans his next kill."

Jordan released a low breath, then eased back a step as if she thought he might use his fists instead of just his words. But he was shaking too hard with rage to care that she was half his size and looked as if the wind could blow her over. Her expression showed concern, but she was too damn beautiful with all that flowing golden hair, he couldn't yell at her.

His friend and the cowboy who'd started the BBL, Brody,

had said she was good at what she did because she'd had problems of her own.

Hell, he didn't care about her problems. He hated everything about this counseling BS.

Talking did no damn good. Only action did. And finding solid evidence that would put Dugan away for good.

Evidence that he might have if the sadistic monster hadn't totally traumatized his child.

His gut tightened as he watched Timmy cover his ears with his hands and rock himself back and forth. The poor little guy was not only motherless but lost in a silent hell, and he didn't know how to help him.

Except track down the bastard who'd done this to him.

But worry gnawed at him, unsettling and cutting deeper than any physical pain ever could.

Even if he did lock up Dugan, would Timmy, the kid who liked to chase frogs, swim in the creek and play horseshoes, ever be the same again?

JORDAN BIT HER TONGUE to stifle a gasp at the raw emotions in Timmy's drawing. A page reflecting the horror and violence he'd witnessed.

A page he'd drawn with his eyes closed.

He was desperately trying to shut out the terrible image of his mother's death, but she had studied psychology enough to know that those images would remain with him forever. Maybe he'd forgotten exactly what had happened. Maybe he'd blocked out the trauma as a way to cope.

Maybe he'd even bury the details and memories for a while.

But they were still there, lurking beneath the surface, threatening his psyche, gnawing at his mind until one day they would destroy him.

If he didn't purge them first.

But purging, healing, couldn't be forced or it might make things worse.

"What did the doctors who examined Timmy say?"

Miles adjusted his Stetson. "Physically he's okay. He wasn't hurt, thank God, at least the man didn't attack him, I mean."

Jordan nodded. "That's good. Not to downplay emotional trauma, but physical abuse would have complicated his recovery."

A bleak look crossed his face. "It still doesn't change the fact that he won't talk." Anguish laced his tone. "Or that we believe he witnessed the man slash his mother's throat."

"Are you sure he saw her actual murder? Didn't you say in the report that you found him hiding in the attic?"

Miles cut his eyes toward hers. "He was hiding, yes, but he had blood on his hands and clothes." A pained breath. "Marie's blood."

Jordan twisted her hands together. "Which means he either did see it or that he came into the room and found her dead."

This time Miles nodded. "He was in the house. He had to have heard her screaming…."

"I'm so sorry," Jordan said, unable to imagine the depth of his pain. It was bad enough he'd lost the woman he'd obviously loved, but to have his child traumatized and left to wonder if he'd ever recover had to be agonizing.

"Do the police have any leads?"

The ice in Miles's eyes sent a chill through her. "I know who it was. Robert Dugan, the Slasher."

Jordan caught her breath.

"I'm assuming you kept up with the case."

"Yes, I saw that Mr. Dugan was released when another woman named June Kelly was killed while he was in jail."

"A colossal mistake. Dugan probably paid someone to kill that woman to make him look innocent. Either that or he had an accomplice."

"No leads on who that might be?"

"Not yet. But I won't give up until Dugan's back in prison."
He cut his eyes over her again. "Or dead."

Jordan tried to ignore the fear that rippled through her.
Miles McGregor was a dangerous man on many levels.

Dangerous to women because he was so sexually impossible to resist.

Dangerous to Dugan because he had stolen someone he
loved and hurt his little boy.

"You and Timmy's mother weren't married?"

"No," he said tightly.

"Have you considered the fact that she might have had a
boyfriend or lover who killed her?"

A storm of emotions Jordan couldn't define registered in
Miles's eyes. Anger? Jealousy?

"My partner is looking into that possibility, but that's just a
formality," he said sharply. "The M.O. is the same as Dugan's."

"Perhaps another killer wanted you to think that to throw
suspicion off of himself."

He hesitated a moment as if she'd struck a nerve, then gave
her a stony look. "Why don't you let me do my job and you
do yours?"

His accusatory tone cut to the bone. But he was right. She
wasn't a cop.

However, she did understand behavior enough to consider
that copying a well-known murderer's M.O. could cover the
killer's tracks.

Still, her focus was better spent on Timmy. "It's obvious
your little boy is in pain," Jordan began softly. "And so are
you, Miles."

If the man's jaw could harden any more, it would have
cracked. "Let's get something straight, Miss Keys—"

"Jordan."

His eyes carved cold slashes through her. "Jordan," he said

with a bite, "I don't need your shrinking. I just want you to help Timmy so he can move past this, and I can put the bastard that killed my son's mother in jail."

"Really?" Jordan asked with a challenge to her voice. "*Is* that what you want? Jail? Because you look like you want revenge."

He narrowed his eyes, then wrapped one hand around her wrist. "So what if I do? Dugan killed four women, five counting Marie. And six if he's responsible for June Kelly's murder. You tell me he doesn't deserve the same torture he inflicted on them?"

Jordan winced as pain shot through her wrist. The instinct to run from this man assaulted her, but she was not one to back down from a fight.

Or a man in pain.

But she also wouldn't allow him to run roughshod over her.

"I understand that you feel that way." God knew, she'd been tempted to track down the teenager who'd killed her little brother and make him suffer.

But killing him wouldn't have brought Richie back.

So, she'd decided she could do more good by helping other kids avoid falling into the kind of trouble that her brother had.

The kind that had led to his death.

"As a matter of fact, I do understand your anger, but that's not going to help your son." She gave a pointed glance at her wrist where he still held it. "And neither is manhandling me."

A muscle ticked in his jaw, but his dark eyes flickered with regret, then he released her so abruptly her heart fluttered at the missed contact.

"I just want justice," he said in a gruff voice.

Jordan's gaze met his, one brow raised. "And for your son to be well."

Emotions made his taut face look even harsher. "That goes without saying."

In spite of his tough act, guilt underscored his words, and her heart softened. Guilt was one thing she understood. Rational or not, it held a power over you that could cripple you.

But a low sound that bordered on a sob echoed through the speakers from the attached room, and she glanced back at Timmy. He needed her help.

Her job didn't include counseling his father.

But still, she had to make Miles realize that they had to work together.

Miles removed his Stetson and raked his hand through his hair. "Do you think you can help him?"

Jordan nodded and dragged her gaze from his rumpled head. She had no business thinking that he looked sexy right now. "Yes, but like I said, it's going to take time. You have to trust me."

Miles tensed, his body going ramrod-straight. "I don't trust anyone."

Jordan gave him a challenging look. "Then you need to start."

He started to speak, but she held up a warning hand and cut him off. "The mind is a fragile thing, Miles. If you push too hard, you could damage Timmy even more."

Anguish deepened the lines of his face, but Jordan also saw fear.

She hated to put it there, but she had to in order to make him listen. Because there was one thing she was certain of—if Miles didn't give Timmy time to heal, and allow him to deal with what had happened in his own time, he would never have his son back.

And that would only add to the man's already burgeoning guilt and destroy him.

Just as her own guilt had almost done to her two years ago.

MILES TRIED TO MASK the fear Jordan's words drove deeply inside him. If he pushed Timmy, he might hurt him more.

As if he didn't have enough guilt dogging him. As if he wasn't already terrified his little boy would never be normal—or happy—again.

His cell phone beeped the familiar ringtone for Mason Blackpaw, and his fingers slid inside his jacket pocket over the device. Normally he ditched it for a few days when he came to the BBL to help, but there was no way he could turn it off while Dugan was loose.

"I need to return this." Even as he said the words, he felt the censure in Jordan's gaze.

"It might be about the case," he explained, irritated for worrying about her approval. But dammit, he didn't want her to think he didn't care about his son.

"All right. I'll spend some time with Timmy. Are you settled into your cabin?"

Miles shook his head. "No, and I need to talk to Brody." He glanced through the window at Timmy, who suddenly picked up the drawing he'd made and crumpled the paper into a ball between his little hands.

Suddenly he felt Jordan's fingers close over his arm. "You should tell him that you're going to be gone for a few minutes. He needs reassurance that you'll be back."

His gaze was drawn to her slender hand. Her fingers were delicate, long, thin…soft. And they felt gentle, comforting. Something that stirred a yearning he didn't have time to contemplate.

He had let Marie down in the worst possible way. Not just by putting his job first, but…by not loving her the way he should have.

And then he'd gotten her killed.

So he gave a clipped nod, then headed to the other room.

Except for a stiffening of Timmy's shoulders, he barely responded when Miles entered.

He approached slowly, concerned about startling Timmy, then knelt in front of him. "Son, I have to talk to Brody, the rancher who runs this place. You remember him?"

Timmy's eyes looked blank, but he angled his face toward Miles. The sheer paleness of his skin sent another pang through Miles's chest.

"Anyway," Miles said gruffly. "I won't be gone long, then we'll settle into our cabin. And maybe we can take a walk to the stables later and look at the horses."

Timmy's little chin quivered, and the crumpled drawing slipped to the floor at his feet. He didn't bother to pick it up or speak.

Dammit, he looked so lost and forlorn that Miles had to blink to control the emotions clogging his throat.

Jordan gave him an encouraging smile, then lowered herself into the seat beside Timmy and gestured for him to go. "Timmy and I will be fine," Jordan said quietly. "We'll talk for a few minutes, then meet you at your cabin."

Miles nodded, although leaving his little boy made him feel as though he was abandoning him somehow.

Then Jordan looked up at him with those beguiling green eyes, and her plea to trust her rolled through his head.

Dammit, he'd been lost before he'd come here.

Whether he wanted to admit it or not, and even if he didn't like shrinks or counselors or talking about problems like these head doctors insisted, he had no idea how to reach his son.

He needed her help.

Trying for some sense of normalcy, he ruffled Timmy's hair. "See you in about an hour, sport."

His gaze caught Jordan's, a silent plea in his eyes.

She nodded, then walked him back toward the door. "If I need you before we meet up, I'll call."

He nodded, not trusting himself to talk, then stepped through the door. Worry crawled through him as he left his son, but he reminded himself that time was of the essence.

That Mason Blackpaw might have news.

So he strode out into the sunshine and breathed in the clean ranch air. Across the way, he spotted a group by the barn, another set of campers grooming the horses in the pen. Normally the smells and scenery in front of him brought instant peace, but today peace eluded him.

He leaned against the porch rail and punched Mason's number. A second later, the detective picked up. "Any news?" Miles asked, not bothering to detail the subject line. Blackpaw knew there was only one thing on his mind.

"Nothing good," Blackpaw muttered. "We put a tail on Dugan, but the rookie lost him last night. Haven't caught up with him since."

Miles cursed. "Can't we track his cell phone?"

"Working on getting a warrant, but so far zilch."

"How about a GPS on his car?"

"Dugan is smart," Blackpaw said. "He had it dismantled." Son of a bitch.

"Can't we crack his alibi?"

"Working that angle, too. Woman who stuck up for him is nowhere to be found."

"You mean you lost her, too."

Blackpaw mumbled an obscenity this time. "I mean she's disappeared."

A cold sweat broke out on Miles's brow. Maybe she'd run off with him?

Or more likely…Dugan had killed her to cover his tracks.

Chapter Three

Miles paced the length of the porch, one eye catching sight of Brody's pickup truck lumbering down the drive. "Dammit, I need to be out there looking for Dugan myself. He's probably already killed his alibi and looking for some other innocent woman to carve up."

"You're preaching to the choir here," Blackpaw said. "But you know what the lieutenant said. You're too close to this one, McGregor."

"Of course I'm close to it, but that's what makes me motivated. Last time I talked to Hammond, he didn't seem convinced that Dugan was guilty."

A long pause followed, steeped in tension. "That's another problem," Blackpaw admitted. "With the Kelly woman's murder, we both know there's more to the case than we originally thought."

"Don't tell me you think Dugan was set up," Miles growled.

"No," Blackpaw said. "I think he's as guilty as homemade sin. But—"

The sun slid behind a winter cloud, making the sky turn a hazy gray. "There is no but. He killed those women and he killed Marie."

"But what about June Kelly?"

"We're still looking into it." Miles had no answer for that. Yet.

"You know, I did find evidence that Marie was seeing someone. Two men over the last five years."

Miles chewed the inside of his cheek. He'd be a piss-poor cop if he ignored evidence and didn't consider every possibility. "Go on."

"The first was a pediatrician named Lamar Cohen but he's clean. The other man was more recent. Neighbors saw them together."

Miles swallowed hard. So this man had been with Timmy? Had Marie planned to marry him? Let him be a father to Timmy?

"What else do you know about him?"

"His name was Paul Belsa. Apparently he was some kind of wealthy businessman. I don't know what kind of business yet, but he was slick. Drove an expensive car."

Gave her all the things Miles couldn't.

"So let's find him and see what he says."

"I've tried to locate him, but the only number I have for him is a cell with a message that he's out of the country on business."

Dammit.

"It's worse," Blackpaw said.

How could it get worse? "What are you talking about?"

"Hammond…some of the guys at the sheriff's department, they've even mentioned the possibility that you could be implicated, Miles."

He slammed his fist against his thigh. "Because I was jealous of Marie and this man?" He exploded into a tirade. "Hell, I didn't even know they were dating."

"I believe you, Miles. But you have to see where they're coming from. You have had it in for Dugan for months. He gets free. You're a head case. You find out your wife has a lover, so you kill her in a rage, and maybe kill this other man, then make it look like it was Dugan so we'll put him back in jail."

He closed his eyes on a groan, pinching the bridge of his nose where a headache threatened. Jesus, God. Hammond couldn't believe that nonsense.

Dragging in a calming breath, Miles forced himself to lower his voice. "I still believe it was Dugan or an accomplice. He could have paid someone to kill the Kelly woman, then either one of them could have murdered Marie."

"True, but so far we've found no paper trail."

"For God's sake, he was in prison. All he had to do was cut a deal with one of his prison mates." Miles heard Brody's truck door slam and watched him climb from the pickup. "Find this other man, Paul Belsa. If he had anything to do with Marie's death, I want him to pay. If not, maybe he can clear my damn name." He wheezed a breath. "Better yet, I'll track down the bastard."

"The hell you will," Blackpaw muttered. "I don't want Hammond on my butt because we talked and you went off half-cocked—"

"I'm not going off half-cocked," Miles growled. "But I need to do something besides sit here and let Dugan get away."

"You are doing something," Blackpaw said. "You're taking care of your child. That boy needs you. So trust me to work the investigation."

Miles's chest ached. "Timmy needs his mother's killer in jail."

A heartbeat passed, the tension rippling between them.

"Yes, but he needs you, too. I'll clear you of suspicion if you let me handle it." Blackpaw lowered his tone. "Besides, you're forgetting that Timmy may be the key to locking Dugan away."

The memory of Timmy's drawing taunted Miles. He felt so damn helpless.

"I'd like to nail him without using my own little boy," Miles said. And spare him the pain of confronting Dugan.

Brody strode up the steps to the porch, and Miles gestured for him to wait.

"Keep me posted."

"I will. And don't worry, I've pulled all the files on the previous investigation into Dugan to see if we missed anything. Maybe he had a family member or an old acquaintance that owed him, and they killed the Kelly woman to get Dugan off."

He'd made a copy of the file himself. "I'll look over them, too, along with all the evidence from the other murders. It's possible Dugan had a partner all along."

"All right," Blackpaw agreed. "But remember, your first priority is your little boy."

Miles bit back a curse. Didn't Blackpaw think he knew that?

Blackpaw hung up, and Miles let his anger go. Blackpaw was right. Timmy was the only witness that could identify Marie's killer. If Dugan knew that and found him, he'd kill him.

And if by chance he was wrong and this Belsa guy had dated Marie and killed her, then Timmy might even be more traumatized because it had been someone he'd trusted.

Staying close to his son was the only way to keep him safe. And Miles would die before he lost him.

JORDAN'S HEART ACHED as she joined Timmy at the small table. Miles hadn't given her all the details she'd wanted, but he'd said enough.

She had also read the police and doctor's reports, and seen the story in the news—Timmy's mother had been an attractive brunette, a working mother who had been raising her son alone.

It was so sad for all of them. Especially for Timmy, to grow up without a mother.

"Timmy," she said gently. "I know you've had a hard time lately." She unfolded the crumpled drawing. "Can you tell me about your picture?"

His big dark eyes looked up at her with a tortured expression, eyes just like his father's, then he shoved the drawing away and shook his head.

"All right," she said. "I understand that you feel sad and that you miss your mother. And maybe you're a little mad, too. It wasn't fair what happened to you and her."

He started a slow tapping of his fingers on his leg, an unconscious movement that indicated she'd struck a nerve. "But it wasn't your fault, you know that, don't you?"

He went so still that Jordan had to grip her hands together not to reach out and pull him in her arms.

"Well, it wasn't. Sometimes bad things just happen to good people." She pulled the modeling clay from the bin next to the table and removed the different colors. "Someday maybe you can tell me about her."

His lower lip quivered.

"But only when you're ready." She began to roll out the red dough. "For now though, we're just going to get to know each other." She eased the blob of blue clay toward him, then gestured around the room at the bin of toys she'd ordered. Blocks, easels for painting and drawing, a toy ranch set with plastic horses, barns, stables and riding pens, puzzles and games and peg boards, and in the corner she'd hung a punching bag. "In fact, when you come here, you can play with whatever you'd like. But today I thought we might work on this clay. Then we'll go meet your playgroup and catch up with your daddy."

He didn't make a move to touch the clay, so she continued to roll hers on the table, shaping it into a ball. Next she poked a hole in the middle. "You can make anything you want. I like doughnuts for breakfast so I made a red doughnut."

He simply stared at the clay while she continued to talk

about other foods she liked. "Ms. Ellen makes the best pies in the world. And she puts ice cream on top. Do you like ice cream?"

He shifted slightly, and she took that as a yes.

"I'm glad you came to stay with us at the Bucking Bronc Lodge," she said. "There are other kids here to play with. We take hikes, and study nature, and have campouts, and ride horses. Do you know how to ride?"

He drummed his fingers again, then inched one hand up to touch the clay.

"I bet you do. Your daddy's a cowboy. He's probably a good rider, too."

He punched the clay with one finger.

"I know he cares a lot about you. You probably spent a lot of time together before you came here."

Suddenly he rolled his hand into a fist and pounded the clay.

Jordan forced herself not to react, but something she'd said had hit a nerve. "Do you have horses where you live?"

He punched the clay again.

"Maybe your mommy used to go riding with you."

This time he pressed both hands onto the clay and began to beat it harder. Over and over until it was as flat as a pancake. She molded hers into the shape of a face, allowing him to vent his emotions.

Finally he hit the clay one last time, then seemed to sag in the chair with a weary sigh. She reminded herself not to push, that he needed time to heal. Purging his anger through healthy means was a baby step, but every step counted.

Jordan checked her watch. "I think it's time for us to meet your playgroup." Jordan swept the clay back into the containers, then gestured for him to follow her.

She didn't give him time to protest but slipped on her jacket, then took his hand and guided him out the front door. The scent of hay, horses and fresh air suffused her, the sound of horses galloping across the pasture breaking the quiet. Timmy's gaze veered toward the stables, the tension in him easing slightly.

As they walked toward the younger boys' bunkhouse, she told him more about the ranch. "We have a lot of campers here," she said. "Some of the older boys came as campers but are now counselors who help us out with riding lessons, campouts and other activities. Last year we had a rodeo and the boys got to participate. We may do another one sometime soon."

He didn't comment, but he continued to watch the horses as if he was drawn to them in some way.

They passed a field where several quarter horses galloped freely, and his eyes widened a tiny fraction. "They're beautiful, aren't they?" Jordan said softly.

A little of the haunted look in his eyes lifted.

Jordan tugged her jacket around her tighter as they passed the stream. "Sometimes we fish here. Then the boys cook the dinner over the campfire. Everyone also has chores, too. Working on a ranch is fun but hard work, and the animals need a lot of care."

Just like little boys, she wanted to say, but she held her tongue. She had to ease into this relationship. Win Timmy's trust.

They'd reached the bunkhouse, so she knocked, then pushed the door open. Carlos, a sixteen-year-old who'd come here with a bad attitude and record, had recently joined the ranks of assistant counselors. "Carlos, I want the other guys to meet Timmy."

"Come on in. We were just talking about our morning hike." Carlos gestured toward the common room where the boys had spread out the nature items they'd collected, everything from leaves, twigs, berries, scrub brush, to feathers and hay.

"We're going to make a collage out of them for our wall," Carlos explained.

Timmy inched closer to her, and she squeezed his hand. Three other boys ranging from age five to eight were gathered in the room, talking and laughing about the hike.

Carlos whistled to get their attention. "Guys, Timmy's going to join us for our activities." He gestured toward the bunkroom. "He'll take the bottom bunk near the door."

Timmy clawed at Jordan's hand. "Actually, Timmy's father is here, and he's going to sleep in the cabin with him for a few days." She knelt beside Timmy and curved an arm around him. "When you're ready to join the boys and sleep in here, you can let us know."

She glanced at Carlos. "I'm taking him to see the horses now. But maybe he'll join you guys later for the sing-along tonight."

She took Timmy's hand and led him from the cabin, hoping that one day Timmy would feel comfortable enough to talk and laugh with the boys.

But as they walked toward the stables to meet Miles, an uneasy feeling nagged at her, and Miles's early comment taunted her.

Timmy had witnessed his mother's murder—and Miles was worried that the killer might track them down and try to hurt his son.

She scanned the horizon, looking for anything suspicious. She'd have to remain on her toes in case Miles was right.

Timmy's hand tightened in hers again, and her heart tugged painfully.

She'd do anything to protect this little guy.

He wouldn't end up dead like her brother.

MILES'S SHOULDERS HAD KNOTTED with anxiety as he'd watched Jordan lead Timmy toward that bunkhouse. Part of him was relieved that Timmy was in someone else's hands for a few minutes—God knew he'd made no progress in getting through to his son.

Timmy barely even let him comfort him.

Another part of him was filled with fear though—letting Timmy out of his sight meant that he might be in danger. If Dugan had tracked them here and found Timmy unguarded or vulnerable, no telling what might happen.

"Miles," Brody said as he climbed the porch steps. "I'm so sorry about Marie and Timmy."

Miles gave a clipped nod, battling the guilt. "Are you sure you don't mind us staying here?"

"I'm sure." Brody propped his wide body against the porch railing. "The reason I started this place was to help kids… and families."

Miles understood that Brody also had his own personal motivation; his brother had gone missing years ago and had never been found.

"I know that and so far, it looks like it's working," Miles said. "But I'm worried about Dugan looking for us."

"I have security covering the property," Brody said. "Besides, no one knows where you are, do they?"

Miles shook his head. "Just Blackpaw, but he sure as hell won't talk. He wants Dugan almost as much as I do."

No one could want him as much.

Except the families of the other victims.

"But Dugan is smart. He may have hired someone to search for me. He knows it's personal now and that I won't stop until I catch him."

"Any leads?"

Miles shook his head. He didn't intend to reveal that now *he* was a suspect in Marie's murder. "He's disappeared. But if I know Dugan, we'll hear about another victim any day now."

"I hope you're wrong, but I have a bad feeling you're on the money on this one," Brody said.

"Did you do a background check on all your workers?"

Brody nodded. "There are a couple of guys with records, but nothing that indicates any connection to Dugan."

The sound of an engine sputtering made Miles jerk his head back toward the drive, where a pickup pulled to a stop. Three cowboys climbed from the inside and strode toward them.

"Come on, boys, I want you to meet Miles McGregor, the detective from the sheriff's department I told you about."

Miles narrowed his eyes as they approached. All three looked tough and rugged, but something else stuck out. They carried guns on their hips.

"This is my security team." Brody gestured toward each of them in turn. "Crane Haddock, Wes Lee and Craig Cook."

Miles shook each of their hands in turn. "Brody explained my situation?"

"Yeah, sorry about your kid's mother," Lee said.

"And the kid," Cook added.

Haddock tilted his hat to the side. "You think Dugan did it?"

"I know it," Miles said. "But he may be working with someone else. A partner or a hired gun."

Lee removed a file from the inside of his jacket, then flipped it open to reveal Dugan's picture. "Don't worry, we won't let him hurt that little dude."

Sweat beaded on Miles's forehead. "I'm counting on that."

He just hoped to hell Timmy talked and identified Dugan before Dugan found them.

Of course, even if they arrested Dugan, his partner—or this copycat—could come after Timmy to get Dugan free again. Or simply for revenge.

HER THROAT WAS SO SLENDER, so sleek. Delicate porcelain skin so pale. The veins in her neck nearly bulged as he tilted her head back to study her.

She had been good to him. The conjugal visits alone had kept him sane.

And the lies she'd told…they had been almost as titillating as having her go down on him.

She moaned and pulled at the bindings around her wrists. "Please…stop torturing me. I need you now."

A slow smile creased his lips as he rose above her. He knew exactly what she wanted. The satisfaction she craved.

He'd given it to her before, even though she disgusted him when she begged.

So like a whore.

She twisted against her bindings, trying to move her foot to rub his leg, but he'd bound her so tightly that she flinched with pain as the rope dug into her skin.

"Thank you," he whispered against her neck.

She purred his name, arching herself like the slut she was, and he slid the knife from beneath the mattress, then placed it against the slender column of her throat. The black gloves on his hands were a stark contrast to her ivory skin as he pricked it with the tip of the blade.

Suddenly her eyes widened, and she shook her head. "Stop playing," she whispered in a raw voice.

A chuckle rumbled from deep within him. "I'm not playing," he said, the taste of her blood beckoning.

She struggled, squirming and moaning, desperate now as if she realized he had used her all along.

"I'm sorry," he said, although he wasn't sorry at all. But his mother had taught him manners, how to say thank-you and please, how to treat a woman.

She'd taught him other things, too….

Her face flashed into his mind, and his fingers tightened around the knife's handle. The other women's faces floated in front of him, a sea of wide eyes, tears and blood…

Excitement shot through him, his body thrumming with adrenaline. With one quick swipe, he slashed her throat.

Her blood spurted like a water fountain, spraying red across the white sheets, across his shirt, across his hands. The scent of it filled his nostrils and made his body go hard. Relief teetered nearby, so close.…

But his cell phone beeped—he'd received a text message—and he cursed, his desire dwindling. He glanced at the blood running down her throat and naked chest again, hoping to revive the thrill but it was already abating.

The need for another already teased at the back of his hungry mind.

Dammit. He hated to leave her so soon yet this might be the news he'd been waiting for.

With blood dotting his gloves, he lifted his phone and checked the text.

Located the target. Let me know how to proceed.

He brushed one bloody finger over the woman's nipple, then lifted himself off of her to type in his orders.

McGregor had robbed him of months' worth of pleasure while he was in prison. Of at least a half dozen more women.

The memory of watching McGregor's whore plead for her life shot through him, and he smiled. Killing her had only whetted his appetite for revenge.

He fully intended to take care of McGregor and his kid himself.

No one would rob him of that pleasure.

Chapter Four

The wind shifted, lending a chill to the air, and Miles jerked his head toward the hill beyond the stables, a sudden prickling of his senses nagging at him.

He'd had the same feeling before when someone had been tailing him, or when he was about to walk into a trap.

He automatically felt for the gun he kept inside his jacket as he scanned the horizon. Acres of lush ranch land rippled and flowed in front of him, the sounds of horses, cattle and an occasional truck echoing in the distance. But he didn't see anything suspicious.

Still, that didn't mean that the danger wasn't out there. That Dugan or his accomplice hadn't found him.

Dammit, he wanted to be working the case. Tracking down Dugan and the bastard who'd helped set Dugan free.

Tense with frustration, he visually swept the area again, but everything appeared normal. He had to trust Brody on this one, trust that his security team would be on the lookout for anything suspicious.

He had failed Timmy before. He couldn't fail him now.

Determination renewed, he took a deep breath and crossed the way to the stables to meet Jordan and his son. Memories of his own childhood haunted him as he let himself inside the barn.

Jordan's soft voice met his ears as he stepped inside and breathed the scent of fresh hay.

"This fellow's name is Dominique but we call him Dom, and this one is Freedom because he likes to run free when he gets the chance."

Three of the stalls he passed were empty, but he spotted Jordan moving along the last four, pausing at each one to introduce the animal and pet it. Timmy stood close to her, his body not quite as rigid as it was when he'd left him. He'd always wanted a horse, and Miles had promised him that he'd buy him one, but he'd never followed through.

As soon as the case ended, he would make that promise come true.

Then he'd sell that house Marie had bought. Timmy would never go back there and have to face the place where the bloodbath had occurred.

Maybe he'd even buy himself a nice ranch, something small that he could manage, a place where he could raise Timmy, where his little boy would have acres to play and roam and explore.

A tall chestnut whinnied, dipping her head out for attention, and Jordan laughed softly. "And this girl, I call her Molasses because she's such a sweet filly."

Timmy actually reached up to pet the horse, and Molasses responded by gently nuzzling her nose against his hand. The sight of Timmy doing something so normal made Miles's chest swell with hope and longing that one day he would have his little boy back, happy and laughing and playing like a child should.

Sunlight streamed through the barn, glinting off Jordan's golden-blond hair, and for a moment he simply watched her, the feminine way she moved, the sultry way she inclined her head and laughed as the horse rubbed his nose against her own.

The protective way she gently laid a hand on his son's shoulder as if to assure him that she cared, that he wasn't alone.

His earlier conversation with her rolled through his head, and he realized he'd been so defensive that he hadn't noticed much about her. He'd been too busy listening to the guilt and recriminations screaming at him, reminding him that if he'd reached Marie's house earlier that morning, Timmy's mother might not be dead.

But now with the solace of the ranch life echoing around them and the sun highlighting her features, her beauty suddenly struck him—not that she was perfect or model-like, but she had a simple, natural beauty that radiated from her, a sweet tenderness that made his gut clench with emotions.

And desire.

He silently cursed himself. Good God, he couldn't let himself be attracted to this woman. She was Timmy's counselor. A woman he needed to help his son.

Besides, what kind of man was he?

Marie had only been gone a few weeks. Even though they'd had their problems, she had been the mother of his child and he'd vowed to try to make things work with her.

Dammit. Her death lay on his conscience like a fire-breathing dragon that had to be reckoned with.

Getting justice for her murder was the only thing that would help.

That was where his focus had to be. Not on the fact that he'd like to throw Jordan down in the hay and pound himself inside her until she made the bad memories go away.

Oblivious to his wayward thoughts, Jordan glanced up and spotted him and gave him a warm smile. "There's your father now, Timmy." She waved at him to come over. "Miles, Timmy was just saying hello to a few of the horses."

Miles forced thoughts of Jordan and her sexuality from his mind. This woman was off-limits and he couldn't forget it.

"Hey, sport." Miles closed the distance between them and ruffled his son's hair. "I know you've always wanted a horse of your own. Maybe after we leave here, we'll find us a spread and you can pick out one."

Timmy turned his small face up toward him, and the hope Miles felt earlier slipped away like dust in the wind. His son's eyes looked so tormented that Miles's gut wrenched. And the fact that Timmy didn't speak or hug him like he once would have spoke volumes for his state of mind.

He glanced up and saw Jordan watching him, and a weight lodged in his throat.

Maybe Jordan would be good for him. Maybe being here at the BBL would help.

If it didn't, he didn't know what the hell he would do.

He couldn't fool himself into believing that everything would change overnight. Not Timmy's condition. Or his own guilt.

And he couldn't forget for a minute that Dugan and his accomplice—or copycat—posed a threat.

That getting sidetracked by Jordan wasn't even an option.

The only thing that mattered right now was keeping Timmy safe and pinning Dugan for the cold-blooded killer he was.

JORDAN SPENT THE AFTERNOON working with three other boys, each with his own set of problems, but not as deeply embedded as the trauma Timmy had experienced. Still, they were here because they needed help.

Rory Morton was eight. He'd been abandoned by his mother, who'd run off to Mexico after stealing money from her boss's company. His father had never been in the picture.

Six-year-old Wayling Gadstone had been abused by his

grandfather, who'd taken him in after his parents died in a car accident. Wayling was now a ward of the state.

And ten-year-old Malcolm Thornsby had been caught shoplifting and vandalizing property with his older brother Jerome, who belonged to a gang.

She let herself in to her cabin, tossed off her jacket, needing to rest a few minutes before dinner. But as always she paused to study the picture of her brother she kept by her bed.

He was eleven in the photograph, gangly, with dirty-blond hair and freckles and a skinned knee from in-line skating in the streets of San Antonio. He had been athletic and funny with a flair for wrapping her around his little finger.

Then their mother had passed away, he'd hit puberty and it was almost as if some other kid had invaded his body. Before, he'd been a feisty, stubborn boy, but the next year he'd turned surly, become mixed up with the wrong crowd and… been murdered.

Unable to help herself, she picked up the folder that held the articles about his death and the gang who'd killed him, her heart heavy as she studied the photographs of the two boys who were responsible.

Fourteen-year-olds who had been trying to impress their leader. Just for sport, one of them had said with a laugh.

She had stared into his eyes as the judge had sentenced him and been shocked at the calculating coldness she'd seen there. At the total lack of remorse.

Rubbing her arms to ward off a shudder, she rose and went to look out the window across the BBL. If those kids, if Richie, had had this place, maybe things would have been different for all of them. Maybe those boys wouldn't be in prison and Richie in his grave.

Wiping tears from her eyes, she forced herself to return to the table and look over the files of the teenagers at the BBL, both the counselors and campers.

Just to be on the safe side, she studied Malcolm's file to verify that his brother Jerome wasn't affiliated with the B-2-8s, the gang responsible for killing her brother. *B* for bloodthirsty, two for the number of kills it took to be initiated and eight for the eight tests it took to join.

The name of the gang Malcolm's brother had belonged to teased at her memory, but it wasn't the B-2-8s.

She spent the next hour combing through the other files, reading through the boys' backgrounds, looking for signs that one of them might be dangerous.

The police had agreed that it was a good idea for her to leave San Antonio for a while. And Brody had promised to check out all the campers and staff himself.

But she still had to be always on her toes in case one of them slipped through.

"THIS IS OUR CABIN," Miles said as he and Timmy entered the two-bedroom log house. "It's pretty rustic but that's ranch life."

A leather sofa draped in an afghan sat in front of the stone fireplace. Beside it two big club chairs looked comfortable enough to sleep in. The den opened into the kitchen, very country but functional, the walls and floor made of knotty pine.

Timmy seemed to take it in with the same glazed look. "Come on, bud. Your room is in here." He gently urged Timmy into the first bedroom with a nudge to his shoulder, then he opened the curtains. The sky had a gray cast, but a dim light spilled in. "I thought you might like this one because it faces the west and has a great view of the pastures where the horses run free."

His own room had a window facing the rolling hills as well, but also afforded him a view of the road leading onto the ranch. He couldn't be too careful. He had to watch for trouble.

Timmy didn't comment, but he did move to the window and stared out at the horses galloping across the pasture.

"I'm going to unpack your bag and put your stuff in the drawers," Miles said. "Then if you want, we'll take a short ride before dinner."

He busied himself removing the few jeans and shirts he'd packed from the house for his son and stored them within easy reach. Then he left Timmy still watching the horses while he unpacked his own bag.

Finally he checked the refrigerator, grateful Brody had had Ms. Ellen stock it with a few items so they didn't have to leave for every meal. A quick glance at Timmy indicated that his son hadn't moved, so he grabbed his leather saddlebag from his Jeep and set his laptop up on the oak desk in the corner of the living room.

When Timmy went to bed tonight, he'd review the files on Dugan's case. Maybe there was some connection they'd missed....

But he couldn't do it with Timmy awake. So he went to Timmy's room, took his hand and walked him to the barn. Timmy watched quietly as he saddled a paint named Spunky, then climbed in the saddle and pulled Timmy up behind him.

"Comfortable, partner?"

Timmy slid his hands around his waist, and Miles's heart stuttered. "That's it, hang on. Now let's check out this spread."

They spent the next two hours riding across the acres and acres of ranch land. Miles pointed out the cattle and explained how they herded them from pasture to pasture to make sure they had enough grass to graze, then explained how the older boys helped with roundup when they needed to do branding in the spring.

They saw deer and rabbits and other wildlife, and each time Miles slowed the horse so he and Timmy could watch the simple pleasures of nature.

"Here's the creek where we'll fish," Miles said. "Maybe we can do that tomorrow. But I want you to join in with the campers while we're here. They'll teach you how to groom the horses, but they also play fun games like horseshoes. I think they even teach you how to shoot a bow and arrow."

At one point, Miles helped Timmy down and they sat on a log and watched the creek water ripple across the stream. Miles skipped rocks, showing Timmy how to angle them to skim the water, but Timmy simply tossed the stones in, seemingly satisfied that the harder he threw, the deeper they sank.

Finally, what little sun was left began to set, and they rode back to the stables. Miles ached for some response from Timmy as he showed him how to wipe down the horse, but an awkward silence fell between them. Although, Timmy rallied enough to help feed and water the animals, then they headed over to the dining hall for dinner.

As soon as they entered, he spotted Jordan sitting with a crew of kids about Timmy's age. He helped Timmy grab a plate filled with barbecue and beans and they joined her.

"Timmy, this is Rory, Wayling and Malcolm," Jordan said, reminding him that when he was ready he'd stay in their cabin with them. "They're going to be in your group so you guys will get to know each other well."

Timmy looked up at them with big eyes, then nibbled on his barbecue, edging closer to Miles as if he was afraid his father might disappear any second.

Jordan met Miles's gaze across the table, the understanding in her expression hammering home the fact that he needed her to break through to Timmy.

Damn. He didn't like needing anyone.

Hell, any time he cared about someone, they ended up dead.

But until Timmy spoke up and identified Dugan, he'd have to allow her in their lives.

They finished dessert and walked over to the campfire. Jordan urged Timmy to join the boys, and Timmy slumped down beside Wayling, but he didn't speak. Wayling didn't seem to notice, though, or mind. He chattered about how excited he was to learn to ride and handed Timmy a marshmallow after he roasted it.

Timmy kept looking back at him as if he thought he'd evaporate, and Miles's heart churned.

Before Marie's death, Timmy had been infatuated with how Miles carried a gun. Marie had begged him to quit the sheriff's office, constantly complaining about how dangerous it was. Timmy had heard her arguments.

Was he worried Miles might be gunned down?

After the fire was extinguished, Jordan walked with them back to Miles's cabin. Before he took Timmy inside for bedtime, Jordan knelt beside Timmy and patted his back. "I'll see you tomorrow. Sleep good, little guy."

Miles gritted his teeth. Sleep was hard for both him and his son—that was when the nightmares came.

He coaxed Timmy into his room and helped him into his pj's and into bed. But just as he was about to leave, Timmy looked up at him and threw his arms around him. Miles's throat clogged, and he hugged him back.

"I'm not going anywhere, sport. I promise." He ruffled his hair. "If you need me, I'll be in the next room."

Timmy nodded against his chest. Progress, Miles thought.

A second later, Timmy rolled over and hugged his knees to his chest, and Miles knew he still had a long way to go.

When he made it back into the den, Jordan was waiting. "Can we step outside for some air?" Jordan asked.

He nodded. He wanted to talk as much as she did.

He jammed his hands in his pockets as they stepped outside. "Did Timmy say anything while he was with you?" he asked without preamble.

Jordan shrugged slightly. "He didn't talk about the murder, if that's what you're asking."

Miles hissed between his teeth. "Then what did you talk about?"

"We played with clay," Jordan said.

He frowned. "What the hell does clay have to do with anything?"

Jordan smiled softly. "It's called play therapy," she explained. "It's a way to allow Timmy to express his emotions. I talked and he pounded out his anger."

That made sense.

"Miles, I need to ask you something and I don't want you to take it the wrong way."

He squared his shoulders. "What?"

"When I mentioned that you and Timmy probably enjoyed spending a lot of time together, he seemed to get agitated and pounded the clay harder."

His defenses rose. "So you're saying that I wasn't a good father?"

Jordan frowned. "That's not what I'm saying at all. It's just that if something had happened between you two, it might help me understand Timmy better. Maybe you had to discipline him or you scolded him, maybe he overheard an argument between you and Marie."

Miles whirled toward her, his pulse drumming. "He blames me for what happened," he said gruffly.

"No, Miles, that's not—"

"Yes, he does, Jordan, and he has every right to." He had to pause to swallow the bile rising to his throat. "I was supposed to pick up Timmy that night to stay with me, but I stayed out late working. I thought I had a lead, but it was a dead end." Disgust at himself made his voice hard. "Instead Dugan was watching Marie and Timmy, sending me on a wild-goose chase so he could murder them."

His voice cracked. "And the worst part is that I let him. It's my fault she's dead."

AN ACHE SETTLED IN JORDAN'S chest at the anguish in Miles's voice, and she couldn't resist comforting him. She reached out and squeezed his arm. "Miles, it wasn't your fault."

His dark tormented eyes flashed angrily at her. "Yes, it was. If I'd gone to her house that night and taken Timmy home the next morning like she'd asked, I would have been there, then Dugan couldn't have gotten to Marie…" He pinched the bridge of his nose. "And Timmy would be safe now, and he'd have his mother with him."

Jordan sighed softly. "Hindsight is easy, but it doesn't help. We can't change the past, Miles, all we can do is work through the grief and move on."

Miles jerked his arm away from her. "Move on? There's no way to do that until Marie's killer is caught. And Timmy is the key to locking him up."

The poor little guy. Did he feel that pressure from his father?

"I know you're counting on that," Jordan said slowly, "but it's going to take time for Timmy to overcome the trauma. And you can't pressure him into feeling like he's responsible for catching his mother's killer."

Miles stiffened. "I'm not doing that."

Jordan reached out to console him again. "I…didn't mean to imply that you were. It's just that kids are sensitive and pick up on things."

"Message received," Miles bit out. "Now why don't you go back to your cabin."

Jordan snatched her hand back, irritated that she'd extended herself when Miles didn't want her comfort.

Miles's phone trilled, and he snatched it up. "I have to take this."

Jordan nodded but waited, determined they end on a positive note.

"McGregor here," Miles said into the phone. "Yeah? Dammit…" A long labored pause. "All right. Send me whatever you find." He ended the call with a snap of the phone, then punched another button and cursed again.

"What's wrong?" Jordan asked.

"Lawmen found the body of the woman who gave Dugan an alibi for the night Marie was killed." Miles flipped the screen toward her.

Jordan's stomach clenched. The woman was naked, her throat slashed viciously, a river of blood surrounding her. She gasped.

"That's exactly the way he left Timmy's mother."

Then a noise sounded in the woods, and she jerked her head to the side. This man, Dugan, was a monster.

What if Miles was right and he came after Timmy?

HE STOOD IN THE SHADOWS of the woods, watching as McGregor and the woman talked in hushed voices on the porch. The kid was inside. Tucked into bed.

Safe for now.

But not for long.

The woman, Jordan, he called her, laid a hand on McGregor's arm, her expression worried. Her voice soft. Tender. Her eyes… almost caressing.

Hmm…interesting.

McGregor's whore wasn't even cold in the grave yet, and he was already working on another. Or maybe she was working on him.

He sensed the heat between the two of them. Just like animals that couldn't stop following their natural instincts.

She was just another slut who would use her body to get what she wanted.

His sex stirred. Hell, how could he blame McGregor? His own body hummed with arousal.

She was pretty in a simple kind of way, not dark and exotic like Marie or the others, but her hair looked silky and her throat…pale and begging to be touched.

He ran his fingers over his thigh, up and down, up and down, his fingers itching to tame that wild hair and wind it around his hand. To tilt her head back and place his mouth on that delicate skin.

To sink his teeth into her flesh for a taste.

To watch the first spurt of blood as he pierced her throat. To smell the metallic odor as it flowed from her body and drained the life from her.

Soon…soon he would have her.

And the kid…he'd take care of him, too. That wouldn't be easy. But he would make it fast. He would get no pleasure from taking the boy's life, but the job had to be done.

Then all his loose ends would be tied up.

All except for killing McGregor.

But that would have to wait. McGregor liked the hunt. The game.

He wasn't ready to give it up either.…

Chapter Five

Jordan couldn't shake the haunted look in Miles's eyes as she walked back to her cabin.

Dried twigs crunched beneath her boots, the wind swirling dust around her ankles. Somewhere in the distance, the sound of night creatures livened the air, but the hiss of cold from the images bombarding her made her shiver with the thought of death.

After seeing that picture of the murdered woman, the one who'd helped Dugan, she understood the depth of Miles's anguish. She didn't know the woman, yet she felt a sad ache for her and her family, and a fury toward the monster who'd butchered her.

Miles had seen Marie lying in a bloodbath like that.

And so had Timmy…

"But why would Dugan kill the woman who gave him an alibi?" Jordan asked, unable to decipher his motive.

Dugan shrugged. "Because he was done with her."

If he truly was a sociopath, that made sense. "Or maybe she realized what she'd done and decided to come forward."

"That's possible, too."

A limb cracked on a nearby tree, and she jerked her head toward the woods. A shadow moved…or had she imagined it?

She paused, searching the area, but suddenly everything

went still. The leaves didn't move, the wind quieted, even the air seemed to freeze as if waiting for danger to strike.

Miles's warning about Timmy taunted her. She had to stay alert.

Deciding she'd imagined the noise, that it was probably an animal foraging for food, she shook off her nerves and hurried back toward her cabin. But each step she took, she sensed someone behind her. Someone watching her.

Something that felt sinister and dark hovering above her as if she had now garnered a stalker.

Clouds shrouded the stars tonight, yet the distant lights of the campfire burning low as the boys settled down for the night reminded her that the ranch was safe. Brody had security. Miles was armed and guarding Timmy.

And she was far away from the gang who had stolen her brother's life.

She was safe tonight as well.

The porch light she'd left on broke the darkness, and she ordered herself to relax. Miles had the sheriff, and deputies were hunting Dugan and his accomplice. All she needed to do was to focus on Timmy and his recovery.

She dug in her pocket for her keys, climbed the porch and let herself inside. But the moment she stepped through the door, she sensed something was amiss.

Instantly, she scanned the den and adjoining kitchen. The books she'd brought to read, the files on the gang, her computer, everything was exactly where she'd left them.

She crossed to her bedroom, and sighed with relief when she didn't see anyone inside. Just her clothing, which was all in place. Even the pillows were stacked on the bed the way she'd arranged them.

Her experience with the B-2-8s' intimidation tactics had taught her to pay attention to details.

They had vandalized her apartment, scrawled graffiti on

the side of her car, all warning signs that she had been targeted for testifying against them, the police suggested.

That was only one of the reasons she'd come to the BBL. But her main focus was not to escape, it was to help other lost kids.

She had to do that or it meant Richie had died for nothing.

Another twig snapped, the sound of footsteps maybe? She craned her neck to look out the window and peered through the darkness, but a dozen different night shadows moved. Horses galloping in the distance, cows grazing, the wind picking up steam and hurling tumbleweeds across the dirt paths.

The ranch housed dozens of employees and far more campers, yet it seemed deserted and spooky tonight.

Then an image of her little brother's face appeared.

She closed her eyes, shook her head and shut the curtain. God help her, she was losing it, becoming paranoid.

She had to get a grip.

Hoping to calm herself, she poured a glass of wine and carried it outside to the porch. She'd keep vigil for a while, chase the ghosts away.

One sip and she tried to relax. She hugged her jacket around her and let the good memories of her childhood back into her soul. The times she and Richie played soccer together. The zoo trip when he was Timmy's age and he'd made monkey noises the entire ride home. The way he'd crawled into her bed when he'd had a nightmare.

She'd promised to always keep the monsters at bay.

But she'd failed.

She glanced through the window at the ranch land. She wouldn't fail this time.

The kids would be up tomorrow filling the ranch with their chatter and laughter, the ranch bursting with life.

An hour of studying the landscape told her she had imagined all the shadows and turned them into monsters. Finally the wine lulled her and she yawned, went inside, locked up and crawled into bed.

But sometime later during the night, she stirred. The whisper of someone's breath bathed her cheek. The husky sound of a murmured voice.

The coarse touch of a man's hand against her cheek.

She jerked awake, gasping for a breath, searching the room. Someone had been standing over her.

The curtain was flapping against the wall, the window open, the scent of sweat lingering behind.

MILES STUDIED THE PICTURE of the latest dead woman, Renee Balwinger, his heart hammering. She fit the profile of the others Dugan had murdered.

Attractive, dark hair, brown eyes, lived alone...

He strode into the cabin, spread out the files of the first four victims he'd brought with him and began to study them, searching for some connection they might have missed.

The first four women:

Sandra Broderick—thirty-four, married once, divorced two years ago, worked as a waitress at a saloon in Santa Fe.

Gwen Peterson—thirty-two, separated from her husband, hostess at a steak house in Corpus Christi.

Eileen Gates—thirty, divorced, managed a motel outside Dallas.

Ruth Norman—thirty-four, engaged, worked at a rental car place at the airport.

Once again, he considered why Dugan had targeted them. At first glance, he and the sheriff assumed the victims were random. They lived in different areas, didn't know one another, did not frequent the same malls, stores or gyms. Their computers hadn't turned up anything either—they weren't friends on Facebook, no business or prior school connection. None of them belonged to a singles group or dating service online either. Even their Twitter accounts, which only two of them had, did not cross.

Dugan had to have met them the old-fashioned way—randomly at their jobs. Which meant something about that first meeting had triggered his interest. Then he'd focused his obsession on them.

Miles took another moment to scan the notes he and Blackpaw had taken on each woman. Of course they'd first looked at ex-spouses, boyfriends, lovers, and although there definitely had been some animosity between Sandra and Eileen and their exes, both due to alleged affairs the women had had, both men had alibis. Gwen's husband had insisted that he had asked for the separation because he'd found a younger woman, but one of Gwen's friends had implied that Gwen had hooked up with another man the day after the separation.

He flipped to the page detailing the FBI profiler's statement. According to their specialist, the killer was narcissistic, had an inflated ego, was charming, handsome and could easily persuade a woman into going with him.

Which fit Dugan to the T.

Most serial killers took a trophy from their victim, creating their own signature. The Slasher had done so by not only cutting the women's throats, but he had taken their wedding and engagement rings.

That in itself implied that infidelity was part of the pattern the killer used in choosing his victims.

Although Ruth was engaged, so far they had uncovered no affair. Of course, Dugan could have perceived her friendliness as flirtation and read her wrong.

Either that, or the fiancé was in the dark.

He massaged the base of his neck where tension knotted his shoulders and shot down his spine as he read further.

None of the friends or family of any of the victims had recognized Dugan or admitted to seeing him with the four victims, and Dugan's name hadn't appeared on a rental car agreement or motel registry. Which didn't mean he hadn't used the services, only that he'd been smart enough to pay cash or use a different name. He had paid for dinner at the steak house where Gwen worked, but buying dinner didn't constitute a crime.

Frustrated, he pulled the file on the fifth victim, the woman who had died while Dugan was in prison.

June Kelly. The same physical characteristics—dark hair, brown eyes.

June apparently lived with her boyfriend, Wally Carlton, who was in the marines and currently deployed. She'd been a single mom, the only victim with children so far—well, other than Marie—and worked at a coffee shop outside of Austin.

According to friends, she had been faithful to her husband while he was overseas, but one of her husband's friends who had recently returned from Iraq had been spending a lot of time with her and her little girl.

Maybe they had passed the friendly stage to something more?

Dugan had certainly traveled around. He probably thought choosing victims from different counties would slow the lawmen down from connecting the crimes, but computers made communication between departments easy.

Still, Dugan hadn't physically murdered June. Someone else had.

Because they'd been impressed with Dugan's work and wanted to win his approval? Because they were working together? Or because he wanted the same glory and fame the press had dolled onto the Slasher?

If the men were partners, the murders could have been a game. They might have even taken turns committing the crimes, establishing alibis for some to throw off the cops, then showing off their kills to one another.

The last file made him lose his breath.

Marie...

His hands shook as he flipped it open and looked at the photo. The crime scene photos were gruesome, almost identical to the other victims.

But the M.O. didn't fit—he and Marie hadn't been married. And she hadn't been cheating. Although she had been dating someone else, which Dugan could have perceived as cheating.

No. This kill was personal, meant to get revenge against him.

Blackpaw's theory nagged at him. He wouldn't be doing his job if he didn't at least consider the possibility that the man she'd been dating, Paul Belsa, could have killed her for some reason and made it look like Dugan.

Belsa could have somehow gained access to the police files or read the trial transcripts and learned the details.

Acting on instinct, he looked him up on Google. He clicked the link to the first website and information about Belsa's business filled the screen, a list of international commercial real estate deals that were impressive.

That must have been how Marie met him, through the real estate office where she used to work.

His pulse drumming, Miles punched Belsa's name into the police database and ran a check on him, but nothing showed. Not even a parking ticket.

That seemed odd, but not odd enough to paint him as a murder suspect. Besides, what motive would he have for killing Marie?

Wiping sweat from his brow, he closed her file, then focused on Dugan. The profiler insisted that understanding Dugan's past would help them understand his motives and catch him. So far, it hadn't worked. And he didn't want to understand why the man would butcher women.

But if he had to get inside his head to catch him, he'd damn well do it.

Next he skimmed the interviews with Dugan. Dugan had been smooth, slick, confident, almost in-their-faces with the fact that he was smarter than the law. He also hadn't indicated any animosity toward women, which Miles had expected to come through. No strict religious upbringing, which sometimes was the case with offenders of this type.

In fact, according to Dugan, he'd had the perfect family. A stay-at-home mother, devoted father, and he was a single child who they'd doted on. His mother had died of cancer ten years before and his father had been killed in a car accident. Neither event appeared to have triggered Dugan's killing spree.

So what had set the man off?

A scraping sound jarred him from his thoughts, and Miles went to the window and looked outside. No cars, no animals in the yard…no one that he could see. But still, he felt as though someone was out there.

The scraping sound echoed again, and he frowned, then realized it was just a tree branch blown against the glass. Suddenly, another sound broke the quiet.

Thrashing. Something hit the floor. A cry.

Timmy.

His heart jumped to his throat, and he raced into his son's room. The night-light he'd installed glowed softly, allowing him just enough light to see that there wasn't an intruder.

But Timmy was thrashing in the bed, whimpering and crying, fending off the monsters in his sleep.

Miles swallowed back the pain the sight stirred, then lowered himself on the bed beside his son and shook him gently. Timmy jerked awake, his eyes full of terror.

"It's all right, sport, I'm here."

Timmy whimpered again, a raw sound that tore at Miles, and Miles stretched out beside him and pulled him against his chest. "I won't let anything else hurt you, Timmy. Not ever again."

His son's tears dampened his shirt. Or maybe it was his own.

Miles didn't know and he didn't care.

He'd do anything to take away Timmy's nightmares. Only he didn't know if he could.

And that scared him more than anything.

JORDAN KEPT AN EYE OUT for anyone suspicious as she and Timmy entered the barn to saddle horses for their evening ride. All week she'd been on edge.

The night she'd awakened to the opened window still haunted her.

Who had been inside her cabin? The man who'd killed Timmy's mother? Was he here on the BBL?

Or what if it was one of the B-2-8s?

Surely they hadn't found her here. Besides, she and Brody had both checked the boys' records for affiliations to the gang and found nothing.

Timmy tugged at her arm, a sign that he was learning to trust her. He still hadn't talked, but in the past week he'd made baby steps, going on a hike with the other campers his age, picking up sticks for the fire and helping her brush down the horses. He'd also regained his appetite.

"What is it, Timmy?" She knelt beside him. "You do want to take that ride, don't you?"

He gave a little nod, then she saddled the two horses they'd chosen.

She squeezed Timmy's shoulder. "I'm so proud of how well you've learned to handle Smoky. If I didn't know better, I'd think you've been riding all your life."

A tiny movement of his mouth hinted that he appreciated her praise, but he didn't quite smile.

"Come on, let's lead the horses outside." She handed him Smoky's reins, and she took the palomino named Winnie. More gray skies greeted them as they headed into the riding arena where they'd practiced the day before.

"I thought we'd ride out to the creek," Jordan said. "We'll be back by dinner and you can catch up with your dad and your group."

Thankfully Wayling had taken him under his wing, and Kenny, Johnny Long's stepson, was here this week, and he seemed to have befriended Timmy, too. Johnny volunteered at the BBL, like Miles, and Kenny had stayed at the ranch numerous times so he seemed to know everything about the ranch and its operation.

She helped Timmy into the saddle, then climbed on top of Winnie and nudged the horse, leading the way. Timmy was a natural rider and guided Smoky to follow Winnie.

Jordan scanned the property, the fresh air chilly but invigorating as they rode across the field, past the stables where Johnny and Brody were teaching some of the older boys how to tie rope knots.

She waved to the group, pointing out that Timmy would learn to tie knots with his own group if he was interested. "Did you and your daddy ride before?"

Timmy shrugged, his little body steady in the saddle. They crossed the east ridge, then she paused to point out the cattle grazing in the pasture. "I think the hands plan to herd the cattle to the south pasture next week. If you want, maybe we can join in the ride."

She nudged Winnie to a trot, and Timmy kept up, but they paused to watch a deer drinking from the creek.

Suddenly the hair on the back of Jordan's neck prickled. She twisted her head around, searching the horizon. Horses... cattle...more deer...squirrels...woods and bare land...

A sound cracked the air, and Winnie jolted. Smoky dug

his hooves into the ground and began to balk. The sound splintered the air again, and Jordan's breath caught as a bullet whizzed by her head.

"Timmy, get down!"

But her warning came too late. His horse bolted, Timmy lost his balance and slid off the animal just as another bullet ricocheted off the tree beside her.

She bit back a scream, panic slamming into her as Timmy hit the ground.

Chapter Six

Jordan's breath caught. *Dear God, please don't let him be hurt!*

She yanked on Winnie's reins and steered her to a tree, then jumped down, scanning the woods in search of the shooter.

Another shot ripped by her head, and she ducked to avoid being hit, crouching low as she rushed toward Timmy. He looked stunned, but he was trying to sit up. A good sign.

Dirt coated his jeans and smudged his face, but she didn't see blood or any visible injuries. Had he hit his head?

She lifted his chin to look at his face. His eyes looked clear, and thankfully she didn't see any bruises on his forehead. "Timmy, are you all right? Are you hurt anywhere?"

He looked dazed, worrying her more, so she checked his arms and legs, but they didn't appear injured. Smoky had gotten spooked and had taken off galloping back toward the stables. "Come on, we have to get out of here."

Jordan took his hand. "Stay low. I'm going to climb on Winnie then pull you up and we'll head back."

He clung to her hand as they ran to Winnie. Trees rustled nearby, a limb cracked and the wind whistled. She thought she saw movement by the mesquites, a shadow. Maybe a person? But he looked as if he was moving away from them.

Was it the shooter? Was he on foot? Fleeing?

Not wanting to wait around in case she was wrong, she stuck her foot in the stirrup, swung her leg over the saddle, then reached down for Timmy. With one swift pull, she swung Timmy up behind her. Timmy grunted and wrapped his arms around her waist.

"Hang on, sweetie," she said. "And lean your head down against my back."

He did as she instructed and she bent forward, hugging Winnie as she nudged her into a gallop. The wind picked up, adding a chill to the cold seeping through her as they crossed the pasture. The gray skies seemed dismal, what little sun had managed to weave its way through the clouds already fading as night set in.

She checked over her shoulder every few feet to make sure no one was on their tail, her heart drumming frantically.

She bypassed the bunkhouse for Timmy's group, raced past the dining hall, sighing with relief when the stables slipped into view. Timmy shivered against her, and she steered Winnie into the pen, then helped him down and climbed down herself.

Justin, one of the older teens, greeted them. "Have a nice ride?"

"There was some trouble." She shook her head and handed him the reins. "Did Smoky come back?"

Justin nodded. "I put him in the stall. I wondered—"

"Thanks," Jordan said, cutting him off. "Do you mind taking care of Winnie? I need to talk to Miles right away."

"Sure." Justin's eyes crinkled with concern. Miles and Brody had both explained the situation to the counselors, prompting them to be on the lookout for anyone suspicious.

She examined Timmy's head and arms and legs but didn't see any visible injuries.

She took Timmy's hand. "Why don't you help Justin while I call your daddy?"

Justin grabbed one of the grooming brushes and handed it to Timmy. "Let me unsaddle him, then you can start brushing him down and we'll give him some food and water."

Jordan stepped aside, removed her phone from her pocket and punched in Miles's number. She tried to steady her breathing but the realization that someone had tried to kill her—or Timmy—was settling in, her fear mounting.

MILES GRIPPED THE PHONE as Blackpaw relayed the information he'd gleaned from Renee Balwinger's file. Renee had met Dugan while he was on trial, then visited him several times in prison. She'd also given him an alibi the night Marie had been murdered.

Now she was dead.

"Was she married? Divorced?" he asked.

"Married. And get this, her first husband was in jail for abusing her."

Good God. "So she's a glutton for punishment."

Blackpaw sighed. "Or Dugan seemed like a prize compared to her old man."

"Right, I forget, he's a real charmer."

"He's a ladies' man all right. A sociopath who looks and acts normal. He dresses well, has impeccable manners, is a successful businessman. He's had investments in several different companies. Women throw themselves at him."

"Yet the bastard likes to carve them up behind closed doors." Miles tilted his hat back and studied the grayish-black sky. "Please tell me he left some evidence behind."

"Sorry. You know better than that."

Miles dragged his hand down his chin. "I keep hoping he'll make a mistake. Any word on his whereabouts?"

"No."

"How about Paul Belsa?"

"Nothing. I checked with the airlines and couldn't find a ticket for him anywhere."

Dammit. This just kept getting better and better.

Miles's phone beeped in that he had another call, and he checked the number. Jordan.

Fear clawed at his insides. What if something was wrong? Had Timmy opened up or had a setback?

Perspiration rolled down the back of his neck. "Mason, Jordan's calling. Keep looking for Dugan and Belsa. I'd better take this."

"I'm on it. I'll keep you posted."

Miles connected to the other call. "Jordan?"

"Miles," Jordan said, her breathing rattling over the line, "Timmy and I rode out to the creek, but someone shot at us."

"What?" For a moment, Miles couldn't breathe. Couldn't see. Couldn't think. "Is he—"

"He's fine," Jordan rushed on. "The gunshot spooked his horse and Smoky threw him, but he wasn't hurt."

Miles loosened the collar of his shirt. "You're sure?"

"Yes," she said. "I checked him over and didn't see any injuries. We rode back to the stables together."

Miles was already heading to his Jeep. "Where is he now?"

"In the barn helping Justin groom Winnie."

Miles fired up the engine, tires squealing and spewing dirt as he sped toward the stable. "Did you see the shooter?"

"No, I think he was hiding in the woods. I saw movement, a shadow, but that was it." She hesitated. "Maybe it was one of the kids target practicing?"

Miles cursed and spun the vehicle down the drive. "You don't believe that any more than I do."

"It's possible."

He gritted his teeth. "It was Dugan. He's here."

"How do you know that? Has someone spotted him?"

"No, but why else would someone shoot at you?"

A strained moment of silence stretched between them as he approached the stables. Then he spotted Jordan by the railing, screeched to a stop, threw the Jeep into Park, jumped out and jogged over to her, stuffing the phone in his pocket. The sight of her pale face made his stomach knot.

Jordan was trying to put on a brave face, but she was shaken as well.

And she had protected his son. Probably saved his life.

He wanted to pull her into his arms and hold her, thank her. Kiss her.

But he had to see his son first. Had to know his little boy was safe and alive.

JORDAN'S CHEST CLENCHED as she followed Miles into the barn. The moment he saw Timmy beside Justin, he raced to him and dragged him in his arms. "Are you okay, sport?"

Timmy looked startled but gave a slight nod and allowed Miles to examine him for injuries. When Miles was satisfied, his shoulders fell in relief.

She was still contemplating Miles's question—why else would someone shoot at her if not to get to Timmy?

"Miles, we need to talk."

Miles faced her, his stance protective. "I don't want to let Timmy out of my sight."

Jordan lowered her voice. "I know and I understand, but you're scaring him." She nudged his hand. "Come on, we'll be right outside the barn."

A muscle ticked in his jaw, but he finally gave a clipped nod of agreement then turned back to Timmy. "Stay with Justin until I get back." He gave Justin a pointed look. "Watch him like a hawk."

"Sure thing." Justin gestured toward Timmy. "Come on and help me with Smoky."

Timmy followed Justin, and Jordan and Miles stepped outside the barn. "What are you going to do, lecture me?" Miles asked, his tone angry.

Jordan sighed. "No, Miles, I understand your fear. Don't you think I was shaken by the shooting?"

His jaw relaxed, a contrite expression in his eyes. "I'm sorry. I…just can't stand the thought of losing my son."

Sympathy mushroomed inside Jordan's heart, and she squeezed his arm. "I understand that, and I am trying to help."

A pained look flared in his eyes, then a second of remorse. "I know, and you did. You saved him, Jordan. I don't know how to thank you for that."

Guilt suffused Jordan. She wanted to comfort him and make his pain go away.

She wanted to pull him in her arms and hold him and…

She could do none of those things. The man was grieving for Marie. "You don't have to thank me. I care about Timmy and would never let anyone hurt him." God help her, but she had to tell him the whole truth.

"I know, it's your job," Miles said gruffly. "But Timmy's my *life*."

She understood. And she had to do everything possible to ensure that little boy was safe. Even if it meant opening up old wounds by confiding her past. "You asked me about the shooting. Maybe it wasn't about Timmy but about me."

A tortured moment passed and Miles seemed to be considering her statement. "What are you talking about?" he asked tightly. "Why would someone want to hurt you?"

Jordan took a deep breath. "Two years ago, my younger brother was gunned down by a gang member outside San Antonio."

Miles stilled, the air growing thick. "How old was he?"

"Thirteen," Jordan said, a knife twisting in her gut.

"Was the shooter caught?"

The teenager's face flashed in her mind. He had the coldest eyes, a face hardened by the life he'd led on the streets.

"Yes, but the police warned me that his gang might retaliate and come after me."

Miles cursed. "So you think one or more of these gang members might have followed you here?"

"I don't know," Jordan said honestly. "But I just thought you should be aware that it's a possibility."

"Does Brody know?"

"Yes." A chill skated up her spine at Miles's condemning look. "He and I have both scrutinized the counselor and campers' files and backgrounds and nothing suspicious has shown up."

"I can't believe you'd come here and put others' lives in jeopardy," Miles said in a cutting tone.

Her guilt deepened, but she stood her ground. "I discussed it with Brody at length. If you find evidence that it was this gang that shot at us, I'll leave."

Perspiration beaded on Miles's forehead, defeat and worry darkening his eyes. Then he glanced at the sky where the last remnants of daylight lingered. "I'm going to call one of the security guards to help me search for those bullets. I'll get one of the others to stay with Timmy. Maybe you shouldn't be around him until we figure out what's going on."

A sound behind them erupted, and Jordan turned to see Timmy behind Miles. He looked stricken, panicked, more upset now than before. Then he ran toward Jordan and threw his arms around her legs, a sob escaping.

MILES'S STOMACH CLENCHED. Timmy was looking up at him as if he was terrified of him.

And he was obviously growing attached to Jordan.

He could understand why. She was kind and gentle and probably reminded him of his mother.

Except she was nothing like Marie.

Marie had stayed at home with Timmy but not because

she'd wanted to. When the bottom fell out of the real estate market, she'd lost her job. She'd been depressed about it and had had a short fuse with both Miles and their son.

Jordan stooped down and pulled Timmy into her arms and stroked his back. "It's okay, Timmy. Everything's going to be fine, I promise."

Her gaze met his, and Miles felt sucker punched at the raw sensitivity in her eyes. Knowing she'd lost her brother somehow made him look at her differently. She wasn't just a shrink; she was someone who'd experienced grief firsthand.

And judging from the way her voice had warbled when she'd confided about her brother, she had her own guilt to deal with.

He'd been hasty in telling her to stay away from Timmy. Obviously Timmy needed her.

"I'm sorry," he said, both to her and his son. He moved closer to Timmy and knelt beside him. "I shouldn't have raised my voice."

Timmy loosened his arms around Jordan and looked up at him, his big eyes swimming with anguish.

"Why don't you walk Timmy to dinner and stay with him while I go look for those bullet casings?"

Jordan frowned and patted Timmy one more time. "It might be faster if I went with you. Then I can show you exactly where we were."

She was right.

"Okay, let's both walk Timmy to the dining hall. He can stay with Brody."

"Timmy's group is going to tell stories around the campfire after dinner," Jordan said.

He gave a quick nod. He would make sure one of the security guards was there to protect them.

He stepped aside, phoned Haddock and asked him and Wes Lee to meet him at the dining hall. When he relayed the latest events, Lee agreed to watch over the group while Haddock saddled horses for them to ride out for the search.

He and Jordan settled Timmy with Carlos and his group. Timmy looked wary, but Miles assured him he would be back, then he and Jordan headed over to meet Haddock.

"How many shots were fired?" Haddock asked Jordan.

Jordan rubbed her temple in thought. "Three, four, maybe. It happened so quickly that it spooked Smoky and he threw Timmy. Then I grabbed Timmy and we rode back."

"I brought flashlights," Haddock said, then handed one to each of them. Miles checked his gun as he climbed on his horse, and they followed Jordan as she led them toward the creek.

Admiration for Jordan mounted in his chest. She had saved his little boy. And now she was trying to help with the case. He tried to ignore the way the wind tossed her silky blond hair in disarray around her shoulders, his body reacting in spite of his better sense. Jordan was sexy and smart and caring…and the confident way she rode in the saddle coupled with the way her butt looked in those tight jeans stirred his blood.

Something that hadn't happened in a long damn time.

Then she slowed her horse to a walk and began to point out where she and Timmy had been when the shots rang out, and Miles forgot about her sex appeal as he began to comb the area for the bullets meant to kill his son.

Haddock and Miles both shined flashlights across the ground as they rode the area, then Jordan slowed her horse, climbed down, tied Winnie to a tree and began to search herself.

"Exactly where were you two when the shots were fired?" Miles asked.

Jordan twisted her head around and pointed to a large rock shrouded by shrubs. "We stopped there and looked at the creek, then the first shot rang out and our horses jumped. We moved over by the trees and another shot pinged by, then Smoky threw Timmy."

Miles angled his head to study the direction the shots might have originated from, then gestured toward Haddock. "Search around that boulder. I'll take the woods."

Haddock climbed down and began to comb the area while Miles probed through the brush near the woods. He found one casing. "I got one. It looks like it's from a .38."

He twisted his head and flashed the light across the neighboring trees and spotted an indentation in an oak, so he walked over and dug the bullet from the tree. Haddock located one more, and Jordan found another below a mesquite near the spot where Smoky had thrown Timmy.

Miles saw the imprint of his son's shoes and an image of Timmy lying helpless and bleeding on the ground hit him, and his anger surged hot and fast.

"I'll send these to my partner to have them analyzed," he told Jordan and Haddock. "If we find this gun, at least we'll have some evidence."

The urge to get back to Timmy made him jog to his horse. Haddock and Jordan turned the bullets they'd found over to him and he wrapped them in a handkerchief. Dammit, he wished he'd brought evidence bags. But at least they'd found proof that there was a shooter.

Only Dugan had never used a gun before.

Although his partner might. And Dugan could have hired someone to shoot at Jordan, then kidnap Timmy.

Another question nagged at him. How about this man Paul Belsa?

Did he own a gun?

If he'd killed Marie, he would have the same motive as Dugan. Miles couldn't stop pursuing either man yet.

TIMMY WAS SO COLD. The fire was hot, but he couldn't stop shaking. The noises...the voices. The gunshots.

His mama's scream...

Kenny and Malcolm scooted up next to him. They were talking about something. The horses. A ghost.

Or was it a monster?

Timmy saw the real ghosts. The monsters. They were all around him. Hiding in the trees. In the bushes. Behind the big rocks he used to like to climb.

The orange from the fire shot up toward the sky. Then he saw the red again. Red everywhere...

His mama's face...her eyes staring at him. Empty. The whites bulging. Her mouth...her lips hung open. Purple and blue...

Then the scream came again. Louder... It wouldn't stop.

Then it was all quiet.

And it was black again. So black he heard the monster coming for him.

It was in the trees now. He saw it before. Today when he and Miss Jordan were riding.

The monster...

It was going to get him and make him dead like his mommy.

Chapter Seven

Timmy's scream jerked Miles from a deep sleep.

A sleep that had been fitful, so he was disoriented when he heard the sound, and for a moment thought it was in his head. He blinked through the darkness, rubbed his bleary eyes, then cocked his head to listen.

A low sob ripped through the air.

His heart jackknifed, and he sprang off the bed, grabbed his gun from the nightstand drawer and raced toward his son's room. Senses honed for trouble, he scanned the hallway between the two bedrooms, then the den, for an intruder, but the shadows from the moonlight streaming through the window proved to be tree branches.

A second later, he pushed open Timmy's door and quickly swept his gaze across the interior. The night-light he'd left on illuminated the room just enough for him to see no intruder. Only Timmy was fighting some invisible monster in the bed.

He left his gun on the dresser by the door, then rushed to his son and eased down beside him. Timmy was thrashing at the covers, kicking and sobbing, a guttural sound that tore at Miles's heart.

He reached for Timmy to wake him, but suddenly his little boy vaulted off the bed and dived into the corner.

"Timmy, it's me, Dad." Emotions thickened his voice. "You're having a nightmare but I'm here now."

Timmy didn't seem to recognize him. His eyes were

glazed, wide with fright, his mind obviously still lost in the throes of the dream.

Or the memory that had imprisoned him for weeks.

Slowly Miles rose and moved toward him, but Timmy shrank back, then picked up a sneaker and threw it, the horror in his sob gut-wrenching.

Miles inched toward him again, holding his hand out, praying his son would wake. "Son, you're safe now, Dad's here."

But Timmy wailed like an animal, and Miles paused in his tracks. A sense of helplessness engulfed him. He had no idea what to do.

Except to call Jordan.

Timmy might respond to her.

He glanced at the clock and realized it was two in the morning and she would be asleep, but Timmy rocked himself back and forth so hard he banged the walls. Miles grabbed his gun then rushed from the room and retrieved his cell phone.

His fingers shook as he punched Jordan's number. Seconds later, she answered, her voice heavy with sleep.

"Hello?"

"Jordan, I'm sorry to wake you, but it's Timmy."

Sheets rustling echoed over the line, and he realized she was getting out of bed. "What's wrong?"

"He had a nightmare and I can't get him to wake up." Miles's voice cracked. "I tried to comfort him, but he won't let me near him. He started wailing and threw his shoe at me and now he's banging the wall."

"I'll be right there."

The line went dead. Miles moved to the front door and unlocked it, hoping Jordan could help Timmy since his son didn't want him.

JORDAN'S CHEST ACHED at the sight of Miles's forlorn face. She wanted to console him and assure him that Timmy's actions weren't personal, that he would work out his grief and trauma in his own way.

But when she heard the troubled wails coming from the frightened little boy, she simply squeezed his arm and hurried into Timmy's room. He looked haunted, his small body tucked tightly into a fetal ball as he rocked back and forth. The painful sounds rolling from deep in his gut were almost unbearable to hear.

She took a calming breath, then slowly walked toward him. "Timmy, it's me, Jordan." He didn't acknowledge her, but she moved closer anyway, forcing her voice to remain calm as she lowered herself beside him on the floor.

Tension radiated from Miles, so she gave him a sympathetic but encouraging smile.

Then she reached out one hand and gently stroked Timmy's hair. "I'm right here, Timmy. And so is your daddy. You're all right now, you're safe."

His rocking motion slowed slightly, and he looked up at her with tear-stained, swollen eyes. His thin face looked gaunt, shadowed by the pain eating at his insides. "You had a bad dream, didn't you?"

He chewed on his bottom lip, another sob escaping.

"Except that it felt real, didn't it?" she said gently.

This time he nodded, a tiny movement, but it was an encouraging sign. "I know you've gone through a terrible ordeal. You lost your mama, and you were scared."

His face crumpled, then he fell into her arms with another bone-deep cry. Jordan swallowed back her own emotions, then wrapped her arms around him and patted his back.

"Oh, sweetie," she said softly. "I'm so sorry. I know you're hurting. You miss your mother. And you learned something that most kids your age shouldn't. That there are bad people out there."

His crying intensified, and she held him tighter, allowing

him to purge his sorrow. "But your daddy loves you, and I care about you, too. And we won't let anything bad happen to you, not ever again."

He clung to her, his little body shaking for what seemed like hours as he unleashed a flood of tears. When she looked up at Miles, she felt his agony as if it were her own.

His jaw tightened, then he suddenly left the room. Jordan wanted to go to him, but she had to stay with Timmy. He needed her more than his father, although Miles also needed help. But he was too proud to ask for it.

Instead he'd channeled his grief into anger and the need for revenge.

Timmy's chest rose and fell on another sob, but his body finally relaxed, his cries subsiding.

"I promise, Timmy, one day you'll feel better. You'll be happy and you'll laugh and play like the other kids." She soothed him with other soft words, repeatedly telling him how much his father loved him and that one day they would have a good life again. Finally he drifted asleep against her chest.

She lifted him in her arms, then carried him back to bed and tucked him under the covers. For a long moment, she sat beside him, stroking his arm, not wanting to leave him until she was sure he was resting and at peace.

When she felt confident he'd settled down, she stood and stretched, then rubbed the knots from her shoulders and left the bedroom in search of Miles. She found him standing outside on the porch, his head bowed, his hands clenching the porch rails in a white-knuckled grip. His shoulders were shaking slightly, pain radiating from him in such strong waves that she felt his turmoil deep down in her bones.

For a moment, she watched him, her mind spinning with the fact that he was the toughest-looking man she'd ever met, that she knew what he did for a living and the sacrifices he'd made, but he was vulnerable and worried sick about his five-year-old little boy.

She reminded herself to keep her distance, that she couldn't get personally involved with Miles. But she had never been one to listen to reason when emotions were involved.

Slowly she opened the door and stepped outside. He was as lost in himself and his tragedy as Timmy had been in his nightmare. Another reason she couldn't keep herself from reaching out to him.

The sky seemed darker than normal, the stars hidden by the ominous clouds, the wind whistling through the trees and tossing dead leaves across the yard.

She took a deep breath, then closed the distance to him and gently laid a hand on his back. "He's resting now."

A long-suffering sigh escaped him, gruff and agonizing in its intensity. "He didn't want me near him."

Jordan swallowed hard. She didn't quite understand why Timmy was shutting out Miles, but she knew it was difficult for him to accept.

"You can't take his behavior personally." She rubbed his back. "You're Timmy's father. He loves you, you know that."

"Then why didn't he want me?" he said gruffly. "He went to you."

"I'm a woman," Jordan explained. "Maybe he associates me with his mother."

He turned his head toward her, and she saw the moisture in his eyes. "No, he hates me. He blames me for not being there and saving his mother."

On some level, he might be right. Timmy was an innocent child who'd trusted that things were safe in his life. And then it had all fallen apart.

But she didn't want to compound his guilt. "Miles, listen to me, Timmy is going to make it through this and so are you."

"How?"

The desolation in his voice ripped at her heart. "It will take time, but you are doing the right thing for Timmy."

"I'm not doing anything," Miles said. "I let him down that night and I don't know how to help him now."

"You *are* helping him." She framed his face with her hands. "You brought him here so he can recuperate, so he can feel normal again. You have me and everyone at the BBL looking out for him. But it takes time to heal."

A muscle twitched in Miles's jaw. "I just want him to be okay again."

"I know." She offered him a warm smile, but a heated moment passed between them, the close proximity of his body arousing hers. He was so strong yet he needed someone to give him strength.

And God help her, she wanted to be that person. To alleviate his pain.

His gaze met hers, something hot and sexual flaring in his eyes. Hunger. Need.

Desire.

Her breath caught in her chest as he lowered his head and traced one finger over her lip. Jordan sighed, her heart pounding ridiculously in her chest. Heat sizzled between them, the air thick with the raw attraction building between them.

His breath hissed out, a desperate kind of groan erupting from his throat as if he was fighting this attraction.

But then he gave in and claimed her mouth with his.

MILES KNEW IT WAS WRONG to want Jordan. Even more wrong to touch her, to kiss her, to pull her into his arms.

But he was a desperate man, and he did it anyway.

One second his lips grazed hers, the next he felt her lips part, an invitation to delve deeper. And he took it at that.

He was just a man. One who had been beating himself up

for weeks. One who knew he didn't deserve redemption, but a man who craved a moment of relief.

Jordan's lips moved beneath his, her hands gently stroking his shoulders as he cradled her face in his hands and deepened the kiss. She tasted like sweetness and understanding and passion, a reprieve from the pain eating at him like a poison slowly killing his soul.

Then Jordan moaned, and her hands trailed up, and she threaded her fingers in his hair, and he groaned. He wanted more.

He slid his hands down to her hips and pulled her closer, the heat in his body driving his sex to a throbbing ache. He swung her around, positioned her against the porch rail, then lowered his head to taste her neck.

Suddenly she stiffened, and she gently pushed at his shoulders. "Miles, stop...we can't."

"We damn well can," he growled against her throat.

"No." She wrapped her fingers around his hands and lifted them, then gave a gentle push to put some distance between them. Just a hairbreadth.

But enough for his common sense to kick in.

"I'm sorry," Jordan said. "I...know you're hurting but—"

"Forget it," he said then stepped back, a coldness suffusing him. "I don't want your pity—"

"I didn't mean it that way, Miles." Jordan's face constricted. "It's just that we both got caught up in the moment. We both want what's best for Timmy, and we can't let it get personal."

"Of course not," Miles snapped. "Now he's resting, you should go."

Jordan stared at him for another moment, then sighed. "Please—"

"Just go," Miles said. "It's late."

Jordan gripped the porch rail and sighed. "All right, but call me if Timmy needs me."

Pain stabbed at his chest. Jordan was supposed to take care of Timmy, not him.

He wouldn't forget it and touch her again.

His pulse pounded as he watched McGregor paw at the blonde on the porch. So McGregor wasn't the saint he wanted the world to think he was. His lover girl had only been dead a few weeks, and he was already rubbing himself all over another woman.

Hell, maybe he'd had this piece on the side for a while. Maybe the kid's mother had even known about it and that was one reason she'd strayed.

Did McGregor know about her secret rendezvous?

Would he have cared?

He remembered the way Marie had looked naked in bed and smiled. He had pictures he could torment McGregor with when the time came.

But for now, he'd follow the blonde.

He climbed on his horse and rode toward her cabin, his body stirring with heat. He'd wanted to draw this out, but after watching her grabbing at McGregor, his blood was hot with lust.

Maybe he'd take her tonight. Have a little fun.

Then leave her for McGregor to find in the morning. Marked and scarred with his touch just like the woman Marie...

Chapter Eight

Jordan silently chided herself as she drove back to her cabin. How could she have made such a mess of things?

She'd only meant to help Timmy and console Miles, but the moment his lips had touched hers, a heat had lit up inside her.

She hadn't felt this intense an attraction to a man in ages.

Maybe never.

What was she going to do?

Nothing. Absolutely *nothing* except remember that she was a professional and that once Timmy healed and Miles caught Marie's killer, they'd go back to their own ranch and she'd have to move on.

Without them in her life.

She climbed from her car, then headed toward the front door. Suddenly the hair on the back of her neck prickled, and she turned and scanned the property. For a millisecond, she thought she saw something move behind a rock.

Shaking off her paranoia, she unlocked the cabin door. The fake Christmas tree she'd boxed up but hadn't yet stowed in the attic mocked her. She had dragged the blasted thing out this year in an attempt to celebrate the holidays. Like others who'd lost loved ones, the holidays always triggered sad memories and depression, but she had been determined to fight it and win the battle this year.

Still, she hadn't had the energy to decorate the damn thing.

It had stood bare in the corner, a reminder of how empty her personal life had become since she'd lost her brother.

She shut the door and locked it, then glanced at the clock. 4:00 a.m. Two hours until she needed to start the day.

She threw off her clothes again, crawled into bed in her T-shirt and pajama pants.

By the time her head hit the pillow, she was dozing off.

But seconds later, a squeaking sound jarred her. She bolted upright, listening. She had to have imagined it. She was dreaming or paranoid from all that had happened the past few days.

Suddenly a shadow moved in front of her and a hand clamped down over her mouth.

Jordan tried to scream but the pressure cut off her breath. Dear God, she'd seen what Dugan had done to those other women.

If this was him, she was going to die.

MILES BERATED HIMSELF for mauling Jordan. She had come in the middle of the night to help his son, yet he'd taken advantage of her compassion and thrown himself at her.

Fool. He'd made a total fool out of himself.

Too wired and disgusted to sleep, he stood and watched the clouds roll in. The howl of the wind mimicked the howl of a lone coyote out in the wilderness and hammered home the fact that he was alone now, too.

He and Marie hadn't exactly had a great relationship, but he hated that she'd died because of him.

Stomach knotted, he strode back inside, made a pot of coffee, then sat down and studied the files on the Slasher case again.

Dammit, what had he missed?

He combed through the notes on Dugan's family, frowning as he reread the interviews. Something Dugan had said once that had seemed insignificant at the time suddenly jumped out at him, and he studied the interview more closely.

Detective: Tell us about your family.

Dugan, with a sardonic chuckle: Which one?

Detective: Come on, Dugan. It says here your parents are both dead. What happened to them?

Dugan: How the hell should I know?

Miles stewed over the wording, then realized that Dugan had asked "which one" as if he had more than one family. But there was no record of an adoption, of a second marriage with either parent, or any stepfathers, stepmothers or siblings.

In fact, in one interview Dugan had painted a picture of the perfect family, one he'd lost tragically. Had he fabricated that perfect past?

Adrenaline pummeled Miles, and he punched in Mason Blackpaw's number.

Blackpaw answered on the second ring. "What the hell?"

Miles glanced at the clock and realized it was only 5:00 a.m. "Sorry, man, I didn't realize the time."

Blackpaw made a gravelly sound. "It's all right," Blackpaw mumbled. "Usually I'm already on my morning jog, but I pulled an all-nighter."

"I hope that means you have news."

"Not really. Thought I had a lead on Belsa, but it didn't pan out."

Damn. "Listen, I might have something," Miles said. "I was studying the original interviews and I think there might have been something in Dugan's past we missed."

"What are you talking about?"

"One report shows that he claimed to have the perfect family. That his mother died of cancer and his dad in an accident. But in another interview when we asked about his family, he said, 'Which one?'"

Once again, adrenaline spiked his blood. "Dugan said it

like a joke, but what if his sarcasm really masked the truth? We didn't think anything of it at the time, but what if he lied about that perfect family? What if he *did* have some family that we didn't know about? A stepfather or stepbrother, someone who might have teamed up with Dugan."

Blackpaw mumbled an obscenity. "You're right. The family we had for him on paper doesn't fit the psychological profile of a sociopath. But if he has a past we didn't uncover, it could explain a lot."

"I can come back and look into it—"

"No, stay put and I'll follow up. I'll call you as soon as I find something."

Miles disconnected, for the first time in weeks energized that they might find Dugan and get justice for the women he'd murdered.

Maybe when he was behind bars, both he and Timmy would sleep again without seeing Marie's blood in their nightmares.

JORDAN'S HEART RACED. She was a fighter, and she didn't intend to let this man kill her.

She jammed her elbow in his stomach and knocked him backward, then rolled away from him.

She slid her hand beneath the mattress, closed her fingers around the handle of the .22, whipped it out and pointed at the figure. "Move and I'll shoot."

The hiss of the man's breath echoed in the air. She had to get to her phone, call for help.

He made a sarcastic sound as if he wasn't afraid of her, and she raised the gun toward his face. Then he lunged toward her. Adrenaline pumped through Jordan, and she pressed the trigger. The sound of the gun firing splintered the air, and the man swung his hand out to knock it from her, but she fired again.

Outside, a noise sounded. A truck engine? An animal?

The man must have heard it too, because he suddenly

turned and jumped through the open window. Jordan was shaking as she chased after him.

She had to see where he was going. If he had a car. A horse.

Darkness washed the property in heavy grays as she searched the backyard. The rustle of bushes near the woods caught her eye. Then the sound of an engine… Where was it?

She was almost certain she'd heard a truck.

But there was no one in the drive. No…wait. She spotted taillights heading up the road toward the west pasture.

Furious and rattled from the attack, she shut the window and made sure it was locked, then flipped on the lamp. She had to do something to chase away the chill engulfing her from the inside out.

For a heartbeat, she paced the room, debating what to do. Was the intruder part of the gang who'd killed her brother? Or could it have been Dugan?

Why would he attack her?

A shudder coursed through her as the terrifying answers trickled through her mind.

Because she was a female.

And because she was working with Timmy.

If Dugan realized that Timmy had seen him and had tracked him and Miles here, he would want to keep Timmy from identifying him.

Calming herself with deep breaths, she crossed the room to her nightstand, laid the gun back down, then grabbed her phone. She clicked her list of contacts, then called Miles's number.

God, she hated to wake him after the night he'd already had. But she had to report this. Tension knotted her shoulders as she listened to the phone ring. Once. Twice. Three times.

Then Miles's voice. "Jordan?"

"Miles, someone broke into my cabin. A man…" Her breath caught.

"What? Are you all right?"

She heard his footsteps pounding the floor.

"I...have a derringer," she said in a shaky voice. "I shot at him and he escaped through the window."

"Dammit. Did he hurt you?"

"No, I'm just shaken."

"Did you see who he was?"

"No, it was too dark." Now that the adrenaline was waning, Jordan's knees buckled. She slumped down onto the bed, massaging her neck with one hand. "He ran through the woods on foot but he must have had a car parked nearby because I heard an engine... I thought you should know."

"Let me ask Ms. Ellen to stay with Timmy and I'll come over."

"No, I'm fine, Miles—"

"I'm coming," Miles snapped. "Maybe he left some evidence behind."

Jordan sighed. She wasn't thinking straight, acting on emotions. "You're right."

"Stay put. I'll be there soon."

Jordan retrieved her pistol and hurried to the front window to watch for Miles. If the intruder returned, she'd be ready.

MILES YANKED ON HIS JEANS and shirt, and hastily buttoned it. He holstered his gun on his belt, then went to check on Timmy. For a moment, his heart tripped as memories of his son's nightmare crashed in on him.

Thankfully he was sleeping peacefully now.

All because of Jordan.

His failures as a father were mounting.

The wind rattled the roof, and he startled, listening again for trouble. But the sound of Ms. Ellen's car rumbling up the drive to his cabin gave him comfort.

He rushed to open the door for her. The curly-haired

chubby woman with her perpetual smile and loving hugs for the kids seemed to have boundless energy. Yet her mouth was pinched with worry.

"You said Jordan's in trouble?" she asked as she lumbered up the steps.

Miles nodded. "She had an intruder. She chased him away, but I want to check on her." He gestured toward the bedroom while she fumbled with her coat and scarf. "Timmy's sleeping. He had a nightmare earlier and was awake for a while, so he may sleep in, but I should be back before you have to start breakfast."

"Don't you worry none, I'll take care of your boy. You see about Jordan. She's a sweetheart, that one is."

He couldn't argue with her there, and he didn't have time to analyze whether or not she was trying to play matchmaker, so he simply nodded again, then hurried outside to his Jeep. Dust spewed from his wheels as he cut a circle in the drive and flew toward Jordan's. He kept his eyes peeled for trouble but the ranch seemed quiet, at peace, everybody and every animal sleeping.

He clenched the steering wheel and took the shortcut off the road, making it to Jordan's cabin within two minutes.

The outside of her place looked dark, the woods desolate behind the cabin. He parked, scanning the area as he rushed up to her door. Jordan opened it just as he raised his fist to knock.

"Are you okay?" he asked.

She nodded, although she looked pale, and he couldn't resist pulling her into his arms for a moment. His heart pounded at the way she shivered against him, a sign she was more rattled than she wanted him to know.

Hell, why wouldn't she be? She'd been shot at earlier, and now someone had broken into her place in the middle of the night. She sighed, shaking, then seemed to compose herself and pulled back. Memories of their earlier kiss taunted him, but he reminded himself not to have a repeat performance.

He was a mess. A failure at his job, with Marie, with his son.

Jordan ran a hand through her hair. It was disheveled and she looked tired.

"Tell me exactly what happened," he said.

"I was asleep and heard a noise," Jordan replied. "When I looked up, I saw a figure in my room."

Miles frowned. "What did he look like?"

Jordan twined her fingers together. "I…don't know, it was too dark for details."

Miles rubbed her arm. "Just think, Jordan. Was he big, heavy, tall?"

Jordan closed her eyes and pressed a finger to her temple, a frown deepening the space between her eyes. "Tall, wide shoulders…big but not fat. Like he was fit."

"What about a smell? A cologne? Cigarettes? Booze?"

Jordan shook her head, then seemed to rethink her response. "Yes, he did smell, but it wasn't a bad odor. It was… subtle. Like an aftershave."

"Dugan always wore a mint aftershave," Miles said. "Subtle."

"You think it was him?"

"I don't know but we can't take any chances." Miles's chest constricted. "Dammit, what if he broke in here as a diversion to lure me away from Timmy?" He dug his keys from his pocket. "He could be going after him now."

He didn't wait for Jordan to respond. He took off toward the door. If this was a setup by Dugan, he had fallen right into the man's trap.

Chapter Nine

Jordan raced after Miles. "I'm going with you."

He didn't argue, simply motioned for her to hurry, and she stuffed her feet into socks, threw a sweatshirt on over her T-shirt and pajama pants and chased him to his Jeep. Within minutes they'd parked at his cabin, both of them searching the perimeter.

Miles climbed the steps two at a time, then opened the door. Jordan's breath eased out when she spotted Ms. Ellen on the couch with a cup of coffee, relaxed and thankfully unharmed.

Which meant Timmy was safe.

Still, Miles slid open Timmy's door and checked inside. Jordan imagined him standing above his son, pressing his hand to his chest to make sure he was still breathing like several mothers of newborns had admitted they did.

Ms. Ellen's eyes widened with alarm as she stood. "Jordan, honey, are you okay?"

"Yes," Jordan said, hating to worry the woman. "We wondered if the break-in was an attempt to draw Miles away from his cabin so that man Dugan could take Timmy."

Ms. Ellen stood, arms folded across her ample bust. "Ain't nobody gonna touch that boy when I'm around."

If Jordan hadn't already been so exhausted, she would have smiled at the fierce protectiveness in the older woman's voice. "Thanks, but we were worried about you, too."

Ms. Ellen fumbled with her jacket. "Don't have to. I can take care of myself."

Jordan did smile then. She wanted to be brave as well. But the truth was that neither of them would be a match for Dugan or his accomplice if one of them came at them armed.

"Has Timmy been resting?" Jordan asked.

Ms. Ellen nodded. "I heard him whimper a couple of times and went in and patted his back and he calmed down."

"Poor little fellow had a terrible nightmare earlier," Jordan said. "I'm afraid he was reliving his mother's murder."

Miles cleared his throat as he stepped back into the den. "All the more reason to push him to talk."

Jordan stiffened. "I told you pushing him could be dangerous. He'll talk, and he'll remember when his mind is ready."

Ms. Ellen gave a nod. "She's right, Mr. Miles. The mind has a way of dealing with things in good time."

Irritation and worry tightened Miles's angular jaw. "Thanks for coming, Ms. Ellen. I'm sorry I had to bother you."

"No problem." She threw her plump arms around Jordan. "I'm just glad you and Timmy are both safe. I'll see you later."

Jordan offered a tired smile. "Remember that I'm taking Timmy's group on that hike and sleepover tonight."

"I know," Ms. Ellen said. "I'm working up a special picnic and treats."

"Thanks, you're a doll."

Ms. Ellen grabbed her shawl and purse and ambled out the door. Miles walked her outside, and Jordan heaved a relieved breath.

But when Miles returned, anger darkened his eyes. "You're not taking those kids out alone."

Jordan hated being told what to do, but she also wasn't a fool. She knew the dangers. "Fine. One of Brody's security guards can accompany us."

"No, I'm going," Miles stated in a gruff voice.

Jordan rubbed at her neck muscles. Lack of sleep and the day's scary events had drained her energy. "Fine." It was still dark outside, but soon the sun would be weaving through the gray clouds signaling morning. "I'm going back to grab a couple of hours of sleep. I'll see you this afternoon."

Miles caught her arm before she could leave. "You're not going to your place alone."

Jordan's gaze met his, her body tingling at the stark protectiveness in his eyes. "Timmy needs you here. I'll be fine."

"I said you're not going." His gruff voice hardened to steel. "You can lie down in my bed. I'll take the couch."

A shiver rippled through Jordan at the idea of sleeping in Miles's bed. Images of him lying beneath the sheets with her followed, taunting her with what-ifs.

What if they got naked and made love?

Hunger flared in his eyes as if he'd read her thoughts, and she forced herself to look away. He was still grieving for Timmy's mother. She was a counselor helping his little boy.

She couldn't allow herself to dream of anything more.

MILES MUST HAVE IMAGINED the look of desire in Jordan's eyes. Although, the idea that she wanted him made his body harden with need.

It had been a long damn time since a female had looked at him like that. Marie and he hadn't been together in years. His job had consumed his life.

His passion had been hunting and tracking killers.

He couldn't become sidetracked now either. Not when his son's life depended on it.

So he jerked his hand from her arm and forced himself to take a step back. "Go ahead. I can't sleep anyway."

"I can rest on the couch," she offered.

"No, go." A muscle jumped in his cheek. "Now."

Jordan's eyes flared with emotions he didn't want to take

the time to decipher. He needed her out of the room before he grabbed her again and kissed her the way his body was craving.

She either sensed he was on the brink of losing control or she thought he was a bastard because she disappeared into his room and shut the door.

Frustrated, he scrubbed a hand down his jaw. Images of Jordan lying in his bed teased him, tempting him to change his mind and join her, but he forced himself to step outside. He automatically felt inside his jacket for his gun as he settled down into one of the porch chairs and studied the woods nearby.

The ranch usually offered him peace, but in the early-morning hours with storm clouds threatening and the memory of the fear that had clawed at him when Jordan had called fresh in his head, peace eluded him.

He wouldn't rest until Dugan and his accomplice were caught and in jail.

Or dead.

He would prefer the latter. The cold-blooded killer didn't deserve to stay on this earth alive.

His cell phone vibrated inside his shirt, and he reached inside and removed it. When he saw Blackpaw's name on the caller ID screen, he immediately connected the call.

"It's McGregor. What's up?"

"I may have something."

Miles perked up. "What?"

"I looked back through the prison's visitor's log and it looks like Dugan had a repeated visitor, but his name had been erased. I'm going to the prison this morning to talk to his cell mate and see what I can find out."

Miles's heart raced. "I'll meet you there."

"What about Timmy?"

Miles stewed for a minute, guilt eating at him like a festering sore. But he felt out of control doing nothing here. He couldn't help Timmy. Dugan was out there hunting for another victim. And either he or his accomplice—which he was almost sure now was an accomplice, not a copycat—had broken in and threatened Jordan.

The sooner he found how the accomplice and Dugan were connected, the sooner he could end this nightmare. If Dugan and his partner were in jail, maybe Timmy would feel safe enough to talk again.

"I'll ask one of the security guards to watch him while I'm gone. This might be the lead we need." And if the man refused to talk, he'd find a way to pound the truth out of him.

JORDAN INHALED MILES'S manly scent the moment her head hit the pillow. She didn't bother to undress; she crawled beneath the covers, exhausted from the night's ordeal.

But images of Miles sliding beneath the covers teased her mind. Did he wear boxers or briefs?

She toyed with the question, imagining him in both for a few minutes before she ordered her mind to regroup. She had taught other people how to control their emotions, how to compartmentalize, and she had to do the same.

Miles was off-limits. When he found this killer and Timmy had healed, she'd never see them again. She was way too smart to try to play substitute mother and wife or lover to a man whose heart lay with another woman.

Finally fatigue claimed her, and she fell into a deep sleep, so deep she barely heard the door squeak open. She managed to get one eye open, then felt the covers being pulled back. Then she spotted Timmy and patted the bed. "Want to climb in and sleep with me for a while, sweetie?"

He nodded, then climbed up beside her. She opened her arms and he curled up beside her. Her heart ached as she felt his small body shudder. She wondered if he'd had another nightmare, but she knew he probably needed sleep and so did she, so she simply held him close and let him snuggle up to her instead of pushing him to talk.

God, she was starting to love this child.

She fell asleep again, a more restful sleep this time, and dreamed that she lived on a ranch and had a family of her own. A sweet little boy and a man who cared about them both.

When she woke up later, she felt as if somebody was watching her, and fear snapped through her veins. She jerked her eyes open, then her heart jolted when she saw Miles standing above the bed.

Loneliness etched his face, sadness and longing echoing in his labored breathing.

"He won't let me comfort him," he said gruffly.

Jordan's chest squeezed. More than anything she wanted to wrap her arms around this big strong man.

Forgetting all the reasons she shouldn't touch him, she eased Timmy away from her, tucked him back under the covers, then rose and moved toward him. "Miles, it's not you," she whispered, not wanting to wake Timmy. "He probably just misses his mother."

Miles dropped his head forward, his shoulders slumped. His whole body looked weary. "But I'm his father. I should be able to do something for him."

"You are." She reached up and raked a strand of hair from his forehead. "You love him and you brought him here. Sometimes helping someone means asking others for help."

His dark eyes bored into hers. "He must hate me. I wasn't there… I let him down."

"You aren't letting him down now." Jordan drew him into her arms and held him. At first he resisted, but then he collapsed against her. For a long time she simply hugged him and stroked his back, but the heat between them began to simmer, the air hot, steeped in hunger.

Well aware his son was in the room and that it was wrong, she finally moved away. Sunlight was fighting its way through the curtains, the hues of gray mingling with golden rays that shouted that it was morning.

And time for her to return to her place.

"I'm going to my cabin to shower." Jordan headed toward the door.

"Wait. I'll get one of the security guards to accompany you and stand guard."

"It's daylight now," Jordan said. "I'll be fine. If I need you, I'll call."

Miles walked her to the door. "Jordan...thanks for tonight."

Jordan licked her dry lips. "I didn't do anything, Miles."

"Yes, you did. You made Timmy feel better...and me. You made me feel better."

Jordan squeezed his hand. "We will get through this, and Timmy will be okay. I promise."

"I hope you're right." His jaw flexed. "My friend Mason Blackpaw. I'm meeting him around noon at the prison to question Dugan's old cell mate. It appears he had a visitor that we didn't know about."

"You think it was someone who helped him?"

"It's possible. We're going to see if we can track him down."

"Okay. I'll take care of Timmy."

Miles reached out and rubbed her arms. "Thanks. I'm also going to ask one of Brody's security guards to stay with you and the group on your hike."

Jordan wanted to protest. But she'd be foolish to when someone had broken in her place tonight.

She cared too much about Timmy to allow her pride to get in the way. Richie's death had taught her about evil.

It could find you and touch you even when you thought it couldn't.

FOUR HOURS LATER, Miles stared at the man who had shared a cell with Dugan. His hands knotted into fists to keep from choking him.

Billy Roeder was a fighter with mean scars, grisly tattoos and a gut that he probably used to help him fend off attackers like a sumo wrestler.

He was also dumb as a rock.

"I told you, me and that pantywaist didn't talk. Night one, I let him know who was boss of the cell."

So Dugan had been afraid of the man? Or had it been the other way around? Sometimes looks were deceiving.

"He didn't mention any old friends that might help him out?" Blackpaw asked calmly.

Roeder shook his balding head. "All he did was brag about his money, his fancy lawyers and the women chasing him."

"What about a girlfriend or lover that he seemed to care about?"

One of the man's eyes twitched. "Had one that came. Heard she was dead."

Renee Balwinger.

Miles leaned forward, arms braced on the table, his anger barely in check. "What about family? Did he mention any siblings, a half brother or cousin maybe?"

Roeder tipped his chair back, his expression condescending. "What about me and the creep not being friends do you not understand?"

"You shared a cell with him, Roeder. You must know something."

"I already talked to the cops a dozen times. Ask them."

"But you didn't tell them anything."

The guard at the door cleared his throat, and Roeder cut his eyes over his shoulder, his eye twitching again. Miles frowned, suddenly suspicious.

Roeder was trying to tell him something. Only he didn't want the guard to hear it.

Then it hit him.

The person who had erased the name from the visitor's log—the one who had covered for Dugan—it had to be someone on the inside. Someone Roeder and the other prisoners would be too intimidated to rat out.

Like the guard with the beady eyes standing watch now.

JORDAN AND TWO OF THE teenage counselors led the small group along the path toward the river. Justin, a seventeen-year-old nature freak who had been bullied because of his thin frame and interest in science, eagerly pointed out the types of plants and trees as they hiked. The boys collected sticks, stones and leaves for art projects and then gathered more sticks for the campfire.

Timmy was quiet and helped pick up sticks although he stayed close to Jordan, remnants of his nightmare still evident in the frightened look in his eyes. He also kept glancing around the trees and woods as if he expected to see a monster rush out to grab him any minute.

No child should have to live with that kind of terror.

Jordan took his hand and knelt to point out the animal tracks along the riverbank. "See those footprints? That means that a deer has been here."

Timmy narrowed his eyes to study them, then pointed to a spot a few feet away. Jordan frowned and noticed that the prints were larger and belonged to a boot. In fact, they were so large they had to be a man's footprint.

She gathered Timmy close then joined the group again. Crane Haddock, Brody's security guard, had been walking along the riverbank as the group sat and skimmed rocks across the surface, so she assumed it belonged to him. If not, there were other ranch hands who could have been out here.

An hour later, they set up camp and roasted hot dogs over the fire. Eight-year-old Rory showed Timmy how to poke the stick into the hot dog while Malcolm and Wayling grilled their own. Carlos, the sixteen-year-old counselor, told a story about the Indians who used to live on this stretch of land, then showed the boys arrowheads he had collected, and told them that they would hunt for some in the morning.

Finally they roasted marshmallows and Carlos played the guitar and taught the boys a couple of songs about cowboys. Malcolm yawned and Timmy looked sleepy, so she suggested they all get into their sleeping bags.

"We'll probably wake up as soon as the sun rises," she said. "That's the way men on the ranch live. They rise with the sun and go to bed at dark because they're so tired from working the ranch all day."

"Come on, Timmy," Rory said as he tugged him toward his sleeping bag. "We're real ranch hands now."

Timmy looked over at Jordan and she gave him a reassuring smile. "Go on, buddy. I'll be right here to watch over everyone."

Carlos and Justin checked on the campfire then settled down themselves. Crane Haddock, the security guard Miles had insisted come along, lit a cigarette and took a drag.

Jordan frowned, remembering the way her father had chain-smoked himself into emphysema. The man's habits weren't any of her business, but still, she wanted everyone at the ranch to serve as good role models, so she walked over to him. "Do you mind not smoking in front of the kids?"

Haddock's craggy face sharpened with irritation. "The kids are going to sleep."

"Maybe so, but I'd rather you didn't."

He grunted, then shook his head as if he was disgusted. He obviously hadn't expected babysitting to be part of his job when Brody had hired him.

"Fine, I gotta take a whiz anyway." Then he stalked off into the wooded area.

Jordan walked back to the fire, then spread out her sleeping bag and sat down to watch the flames. The boys, exhausted from the hike, had already fallen asleep.

Suddenly a noise behind her startled her. Trees rustling? A twig snapping?

Then another noise, louder. Like a man or animal crashing into the leaves.

She swirled around, searching the darkness, hoping to see the pinprick of light from Haddock's cigarette, but it wasn't there. Nerves on edge, she stood and scanned the woods.

"Crane?"

Only the whisper of the leaves rustling in the wind sounded. Then another crack. A gunshot. Muffled.

Fear choked her, and she inched deeper into the woods, weaving between the trees toward the area where Crane had disappeared. On instinct, she slid her derringer from her coat pocket, praying she didn't have to use it. A faint sliver of moonlight lit her path as she took another step, her hand shaking at every tiny sound echoing around her.

Scrub brush and weeds clawed at the leg of her jeans, then she spotted the glow of the cigarette on the ground behind a clump of rocks.

Her heart jumped as she stepped around the rocks and found Crane Haddock lying facedown in the dirt. Had he fallen?

She knelt slowly to check his pulse, her eyes tracking the property and trailing back to the boys who were still nestled around the campfire.

But she didn't feel a pulse.

"Haddock," she whispered as she slowly rolled him over. "Come on, don't do this to me…."

But the blood gushing from his chest told her it was too late.

Haddock was dead.

Chapter Ten

Miles relayed his suspicions to Blackpaw as soon as they left Roeder, and they went straight to the warden.

Warden Everett Case was a tall husky man who, judging from the photos on the wall of his office, had served in the military. But the years since he'd left had changed him from a fit man to one who needed to lose about fifty pounds. Muscle had turned to fat, the steely focus in his eyes in the picture filled now with cynicism.

What if the warden was in on the cover-up as well? He'd met enough dirty cops, judges and prison employees to know that money talked.

"Did you learn anything from Roeder?" Case asked.

Miles shrugged. "Not really. Except we think he wouldn't talk because of one of your guards."

Blackpaw produced the copy of the visitor's log he had accessed. No doubt he'd sweet-talked one of the female officers into giving it to him. "Look at this. Dugan had a visitor on more than one occasion but the name has been whited out."

Case took the copy and narrowed his eyes as he studied it. "So?"

"We think this visitor may be working with Dugan," Miles explained. "And that Dugan paid off your guard to cover up his name."

Case rolled his shoulders. "That's a strong accusation. Do you have proof?"

"No, but look at the date of the last visit. A week before the fifth victim was killed, the murder that helped free Dugan."

A long silence passed as Case chewed over the suggestion. "So whoever killed this woman did so intentionally to help Dugan."

Miles shifted. "We believe they were working together. If your guard knows this person's identity, he's aiding a killer."

Case released a frustrated breath, then pressed the intercom to his secretary. "Tillie, page Lonnie Banning and tell him I need to see him in my office ASAP."

Miles paced to the window and looked out at the yard where several prisoners lingered. Roeder was hunched by the fence smoking a cigarette, his eyes scanning the space as if expecting trouble.

A minute later, Banning knocked then strode in. The guard was wiry with pocked skin and a decided limp. Miles wondered if he'd gotten it from one of the inmates.

His look turned suspicious the moment he spotted Miles and Blackpaw. "What's going on?" Banning asked.

The warden cleared his throat. "These detectives have reason to believe that you erased a name from the visitor log. A man who visited Robert Dugan."

"That's crazy," Banning said in a terse voice.

"Listen to me," the warden said just as coldly. "I know you've accepted bribes and sneaked in drugs for the men. But this is different. The detectives suspect this visitor killed a woman to help overturn Dugan's conviction—"

"I don't know what you're talking about," Banning said.

"The hell you don't," Miles cut in. "Dugan paid you to cover up for him."

Case glanced at Miles, then propped his fists on his desk and leaned toward Banning with an intimidating look. "If you did this, and this man turns out to be Dugan's accomplice, you're going to jail, Banning." A nasty leer carved grooves across Case's face, and Miles realized the weight he'd put on hadn't diminished his capability to enforce justice.

A bead of sweat popped out on Banning's forehead. "I told you I don't know what you're talking about."

The warden made a sound of disgust, then sat down at the desk and punched some keys on the computer. A few minutes later, he'd accessed a file of visitor logs.

Miles frowned. If Banning had erased the names on the written log, he'd probably also done so on the computer version.

"You're not going to find anything that isn't there," Banning said.

Case pressed a few more keys, studied another file for a moment, then pivoted the screen to show them. "You're lying, Banning."

Miles noticed the date and his pulse jumped.

"How… What did you do?" Banning shifted nervously. "I—"

"You thought you erased it, but I had software installed to keep track of everyone who logs into the computer system and exactly what they do."

"You spy on your employees?" Banning asked, shocked.

Case gave a clipped nod then stood. "I'm running a prison here, Banning. Safety and security have to be top-notch." He pointed to the name on the file. *Pruitt Ables.* "So there's no need to deny that you did erase it. Now who in the hell is this Ables man?"

Banning wiped the back of his neck and glared at Miles and Blackpaw. Suddenly a loud commotion broke out outside. Miles glanced through the warden's window and saw several men shouting and jumping into a pile. The warden scowled, clicked his radio.

"What now?" he asked into the mike.

"Fight," one of the guards responded.

A palpable awkwardness filled the room as they watched the scene unfolding. Seconds later, three guards pulled the prisoners apart. Miles's pulse hammered as he saw the man at the bottom of the pile.

Roeder.

One of the guards leaned over him and checked his pulse. "Roeder's dead," he said over the mike. "Stabbed in the chest."

The warden cursed, then turned back to Banning. "You have five seconds to tell me the truth."

Banning paled and swiped at his forehead, then took a step back, panic on his face as if he was about to run.

A buzzing sounded, then another guard stepped in, folded his arms and blocked the doorway. "I mean it, Banning," Case snapped.

"Fess up or I'll arrest you for accessory to murder," Miles said. "I don't imagine you made friends with every prisoner in here. How do you think you'll like spending time in the cell with some of the ones you didn't buddy up to?"

Blackpaw grunted. "Especially now they know ratting you out got Roeder killed."

Banning cursed. "All right, all right. But I didn't have nothing to do with Dugan murdering those women."

"What about June Kelly, the woman whose death enabled Dugan's release?"

"I don't know anything about that either," Banning said in a shaky voice.

"But you covered up for Dugan's visitor, Pruitt Ables." Miles gripped the man by the collar.

Banning shuddered. "Dugan paid me a lot of money to erase the name. He didn't explain why and I didn't ask."

"But you knew something wasn't right," Miles barked. "So who in the hell is he to Dugan?"

Banning's chest rose up and down as he struggled to breathe. "Ables is Dugan's half brother."

Miles gritted his teeth. A half brother that none of them had even known existed.

A man who shared the same genes.

A man who might have killed Kelly to set his brother free. A man who might be helping him track down Timmy.

PANIC TUGGED AT JORDAN as she felt Haddock's pulse one last time. Maybe she'd misread it, but no…there was no pulse. He was definitely dead.

Fear knotted her stomach and she scanned the area, half expecting the shooter to fire again. But a heartbeat passed and danger echoed in the air with only the sound of the whistling wind swirling around her.

She had to get back to the boys.

Adrenaline surged through her, and she pivoted, keeping her eyes peeled for an attack. Haddock had been protecting her and Timmy.

Had the shooter murdered him to get to Timmy?

Her hands shook as she pawed through some scrub brush and hurried back to the camp. She kept her gun clenched tightly in her hand but she needed her phone. She had to call Miles.

A sound behind her made her jump, but she spun around and realized it was an opossum. Another twig snapped from a limb above and fell to the ground.

She stepped on it and picked up her pace, racing back to the camp. Her breath stalled in her chest as she drew near it, and she raked her gaze across the sleeping bags beside the fire. At first glance, all the boys seemed to be safe.

And she didn't spot Dugan or a shooter.

Relief warred with fear, and she forced a calming breath, then strode toward them. The two counselors had sacked out.

Wayling and Malcolm were side by side while Rory lay on his side facing Timmy as if they'd been talking before they'd fallen asleep.

Gravel and dirt crunched beneath her boots as she approached. She leaned over Timmy, relief spilling through her when she realized he was sound asleep.

And safe.

But Haddock was still dead, and she had to contact Miles.

She tiptoed past Timmy, then made her way to her duffel bag and dug inside. A second later, she retrieved her phone and punched Miles's number. The need to make sure Timmy and the others were safe clawed at her as she listened to the phone ring over and over.

Timmy began to stir and she knelt beside him and rubbed his back, hoping to ward off one of the nightmares that haunted him.

Finally after the fifth ring, the voice mail clicked on. She was just about to leave a message, then phone Brody, when suddenly a limb cracked behind her. The scent of the firewood mingled with something else—a man's cologne.

She spun around and saw a shadow hovering above her, then suddenly a hard hand reached out and grabbed the phone away from her. A firm arm slid around her neck and he jerked her head backward.

"Hello, Jordan. Give me the gun, or Timmy's dead."

THE EXCITEMENT OF FINALLY having a clue zinged through Miles. If he could find Ables, he might be able to prove he'd been working with Dugan. Or at least that he had killed June Kelly and that Dugan had been guilty of the other murders and belonged on death row.

"Thank you, Warden." Miles shook the man's hand. "This could be the missing link to this case."

"I hope you find the SOB," Case said. "I've seen a lot

of men go through this place. Most guilty, although a few I thought might have been wrongly incarcerated. Dugan wasn't one of them."

"You believed he was guilty?" Miles asked.

Case nodded. "He was too slick. Too composed. If you ask me, he's a sociopath."

Which meant he had no conscience. That it hadn't fazed him to kill the women.

And it wouldn't bother him to take away his son's life either.

Cold fear knotted Miles's belly.

"Excuse me, I need to check on my son." He turned to Blackpaw. "And let's find out everything we can on Pruitt Ables."

"I'll call in a favor to an FBI agent I know. If anyone can dig up information about Ables, he can."

Miles thanked him and the two of them worked their way back through security. By the time Miles stepped outside into the fresh air, he noticed Jordan had called. She hadn't left a message, but still, alarm rippled through him and he punched her number. Mason called his friend as Miles walked to his Jeep.

The phone trilled and trilled but Jordan didn't answer. Miles checked the time on his phone. Eight forty-five. She had taken the group for a hike and they were camping outdoors, but they should be settled down by now.

And why hadn't she left a message?

The sky was growing darker. The boys might be asleep but Jordan probably wasn't.

His nerves kicked in and he tried Haddock's number, but it rolled to voice mail, too. Anxiety knotted his insides. One of them should be answering.

He jumped into his Jeep. "Let's go. Jordan's not answering and neither is the security guard that's supposed to be watching her and the kids."

Mason slanted him a concerned look, then Miles started the engine and peeled away from the prison. He tried Jordan again, but once more her message machine clicked on.

"Jordan, I'm on my way back, but I'm worried. Call me as soon as you get this."

He sped up, the Jeep eating the distance, his fear mounting with each mile marker they passed.

If anything happened to Timmy, he'd never forgive himself. And what about Jordan? What if Dugan had hurt her?

Images of the dead women, of Marie butchered, haunted him.

Trembling with fear, he punched Brody's number, tapping his fingers on the door as he waited. By the time Brody answered, he thought his head was going to explode.

"Brody, have you heard from Jordan or Haddock lately?"

"No," Brody said. "Why?"

"I've tried both their phones but they keep going to voice mail."

Brody made a clicking sound with his teeth. "Maybe they turned them off to sleep."

"Haddock is supposed to be on duty. He should be available."

Brody mumbled agreement. "I'm on my way home from town, but if you're worried, I'll call Wes Lee and ask him to ride out there."

"Thanks," Miles said. "I'll be there as soon as possible."

Miles ended the call, his heart drumming as he sped up again.

If Dugan or this Ables man had hurt Timmy, he'd forget jail. He'd kill the bastard and put him in the ground himself.

JORDAN'S HEART SPUTTERED as Dugan gripped her neck tighter. She'd heard her cell phone ringing a minute ago. It was probably Miles checking in.

She had to stall. If she didn't answer, he'd send someone to check on them. Struggling for courage, she tried to sound calm. Reason with the man. "There's no reason to hurt that little boy, Dugan."

"Aah, so you do know my name."

"Yes, and you're taking a terrible chance being here, especially if you're innocent like you say. Or have you decided to confess?"

"Now, why would I want to do a stupid thing like that when I'm innocent?" Dugan murmured against her ear.

"You like to hurt women," Jordan said, her voice hoarse from the way his hand was cutting off her windpipe.

"Women come on to me," Dugan said with a brittle laugh. "Can I help it if I'm charming?"

"A charming, *innocent* man wouldn't be holding me hostage right now," Jordan quipped. "Or threatening to hurt a five-year-old little boy."

He jerked her around to face him, his eyes wild. Jordan had seen pictures of him in his slick suits, his manicured nails, his polished expressions, and wondered if he had been innocent or guilty. If the police could have been wrong.

But the dark, sinister glint in his eyes indicated he was every bit the cunning, methodical sociopath Miles had painted him to be.

The sound of a horse echoed in the night, and Jordan froze, praying it was Miles. Then again, if he approached them, Dugan might kill him.

Dugan must have heard the horse too, because he dragged her back into the shadows of a tree and tightened his hold.

"You might as well give it up, Dugan," Jordan said, fighting panic. "You're not going to get away with this."

"Oh, I have plans," he said in that same low murmur. "Plans for you and the boy. And nobody is getting in my way."

The horse slowed, and Jordan squinted to see who was climbing off.

Not Miles, but Wes Lee, one of the other security guards. Miles must have asked him to check things out.

"Haddock," Lee called as he strode toward the campsite. "Where are you? Brody called and said Miles has been calling you and Jordan."

Jordan tried to warn him. "Watch out—"

Dugan slammed his fist against her head, and she sank to the ground. A second later, a shot rang out.

Tears and blood trickled into her eyes as she tried to lift herself up to fight back. Then Lee collapsed onto the ground, and she choked back a scream.

Lee was shot. Maybe dead.

God help her. She had to figure out a way to save Timmy and the other boys herself.

She struggled to stand up, but her head spun, then Dugan punched her again. She staggered, gasping for a breath, so dizzy she felt sick. Before she could recover, he yanked her arms behind her and tied them together, then shoved her up against the tree.

He'd said he had plans for her and Timmy.

He had tortured and raped the other women he was accused of killing before he'd viciously slashed their throats.

Was that what he had planned for her?

And after he killed her, would he kill Timmy, too?

Chapter Eleven

Jordan swallowed back her fear. She would not let this man get inside her head. He thrived on terrorizing women, so showing him she wasn't afraid was the only way to win.

The night sky twirled sickeningly as he strode over to Lee, kicked his gun away, then checked her phone.

A cry caught in her throat as he scrolled down her caller log. He was going to let Miles know he was here. That he had her.

Because more than anything the madman wanted Miles to suffer.

She struggled with her bindings, determined to free herself and protect the kids, but Dugan turned, his eyes boring into hers, and she stilled. She had to play this smart.

Get inside his head instead of letting him intimidate her. She didn't have his physical strength, but she could use her skills to talk to him, maybe convince him that hurting Timmy wasn't the answer.

After all, he was deviating from his pattern. Dugan killed women for the pleasure of it. Probably because of something that had happened in his past.

But killing children wasn't part of his M.O.

The situation had changed, she reminded herself. Timmy had witnessed his mother's murder. That detail differed from the other murders. There had been no witnesses. No kids around.

No one left behind to identify him.

Although by coming after Timmy, Dugan only made himself look guilty. And who knew if Timmy would ever remember or be able to testify...

Something had triggered Dugan to veer from his usual methodical, cunning, well-planned attacks, to escalate enough to take chances. Which meant he was out of control.

And even more dangerous.

She shifted, working the ropes binding her against a rock. The stone jabbed her fingers, scraped at her skin, and she felt a drop of blood roll down her palm. Dugan twisted to watch her, and she forced herself to be still.

She needed to keep him talking. Stalling might give Miles and Brody enough time to devise a rescue plan.

But in spite of her bravado, Dugan strode over, knelt beside her and waved a knife in front of her face as he punched in a phone number. Fear crawled through her.

If he was out of control, he might kill them all, and she couldn't stop him.

MILES WAS SWEATING BULLETS by the time they made it back to the BBL. Just as he swerved into the drive to the main ranch house, his cell phone trilled.

Miles flipped it to check the caller ID, his heart pounding when he spotted Jordan's name. Dammit. Maybe he'd panicked for nothing.

But the moment he connected the call, a bad feeling pinched his gut. It wasn't Jordan's voice, but a low breathing.

"Jordan?" Miles said. "Are you there?"

"Oh, she's here." A sinister laugh echoed back. A voice he recognized as Dugan.

He closed his eyes and gripped the seat edge, grappling

for control and praying at the same time. "If you hurt her or my little boy, I'll kill you with my bare hands."

Another laugh, loud and long this time. "Careful now. You are a man of the law, McGregor."

Mason was looking his way, his brows raised in question.

Miles jumped from the Jeep and paced back and forth. "I don't give a damn about the law right now."

"But you do want your son back, don't you?" Dugan asked.

Miles motioned for Mason to park at the house. He'd get Brody and the others and they'd surround the ranch if they needed to. "Let me talk to Timmy," Miles snapped.

"I'm afraid that's not possible."

Miles's heart stopped. No... "What?"

Dugan laughed coyly. "The kid is sleeping, but guess who I have right beside me?"

"Miles," Jordan yelled. "He killed Haddock—"

Her voice was cut off as a loud smack echoed over the line. Miles's blood ran cold as he realized Dugan had hit Jordan.

What else had he done to her? What else would he do?

His stomach knotted.

"You son of a bitch," Miles growled. "Let Jordan and the kids go. It's me you want, not them."

"Aah, but I have you now," Dugan said smugly.

The sadistic bastard. "Come on, Dugan. You don't hurt kids, that's not what you enjoy."

"I'm enjoying myself now."

Miles silently cursed. Yeah, Dugan was having fun. He wanted him squirming. Worrying. Terrified.

And he was right—the best way to accomplish that was to threaten Timmy.

"You won't get off this ranch alive," Miles said. "I promise you that."

"Tsk, tsk, tsk, Detective. Don't make promises you can't keep."

"I will keep this one," Miles said through gritted teeth.

"I'm sure you promised your son's mama you'd take care of her, too. And little Timmy here, I bet you told him the same thing." He paused, his voice almost singsongy as if he was playing a game. "And look how that worked out."

Miles opened his mouth to try to reason with the bastard, but the phone clicked dead. He cursed and slammed it against his leg.

"What did he say?" Mason asked.

"He killed Haddock, and he has Jordan and Timmy."

"Hell."

Miles called Brody to fill him in. "Dugan's on the ranch," he told Brody. "He killed Haddock, and he has Jordan and Timmy's group."

Brody released a string of expletives. "What about Wes Lee? I sent him out to check on them."

"I don't know," Miles said, although his gut told him Lee was probably dead as well. Dugan was definitely demented. He didn't care who knew he was guilty. His focus was to torture Miles, and he was killing anyone who got in his way.

Timmy's sweet little face flashed in his mind. No...he couldn't lose him.

Maybe Jordan could save him...keep Dugan occupied until they could corner him.

But terror and doubt still nagged at him. But what if he killed her first?

She had done nothing wrong. Nothing except help Timmy.

And now she might end up dead like Marie because of it.

JORDAN BREATHED THROUGH the panic eating at her. She had to stay calm. Climb into Dugan's head.

He stowed the knife but waved his gun at her. "Get the kids up. We need to move."

"What are you talking about?" Jordan asked. "They're sleeping."

His eyes turned wild. "We're too out in the open here." He shoved the gun at her side. "Now move it."

Jordan winced as he gripped her arm, forced her to stand and shoved her forward. She staggered and stumbled over a rock, and he cursed.

"Don't even think about running." The barrel of his weapon dug into her side. "If you do, I'll kill one of the boys."

Jordan bit her tongue to suppress a gasp, then faced him with her chin held high. "I'm not running, but I can't walk straight with you shoving me around. If you want me to move the boys, let me do it my way or you'll have some hysterical, angry kids on your hands, and that could mean trouble for all of us."

His sinister gaze met hers, and she could have sworn she saw admiration flicker in his eyes. "All right, but I'm warning you. I will punish you if you disobey me."

"Is that what your mother did to you?" Jordan asked.

His lips thinned, all charm fading from his fake smiles. "Don't talk to me about my mother."

A small sense of victory niggled at her. Maybe she'd hit on the crux of Dugan's problem. If so, she could use that information to reach him.

"Listen to me," Jordan said. "I want to see everyone leave this situation safely. Especially these innocent children." She released a pent-up breath. "So if you stay calm and don't hurt them, I'll help you figure out a way to escape before the cops come." She looked him square in the eye. "Because you know they will eventually catch up with you, and then you're going to wind up back in jail or…dead yourself."

He gripped her arm so tightly pain shot up her arm. "Don't threaten me—"

"I'm not," Jordan said quietly. "But I don't believe you want to hurt these boys. You may not like women, but think about it. These kids are just like you were when you were little. They're young and they've already had a boatload of trouble and bad people in their lives. You don't want to add to that."

He cursed and released her arm so viciously she stumbled again. "Stop talking and get them moving. *Now.*"

"Untie me first so they don't freak out when they see me."

He studied her for a long minute, then gave a clipped nod. "But remember. If you try anything, I'll shoot one of them."

Jordan gave him a short nod, then made her way to the two counselors first. She gently nudged Justin awake, then kept her voice low. "Justin, we have a problem. That man Miles was worried about is here and he has a gun." Justin looked up at her in a sleepy haze, but worry creased his forehead as her words registered.

"He—"

"Yes, he's armed," she said quietly. "But I don't want to frighten the boys. So help me wake them." She took his hand and helped him stand, carefully planting herself between him and Dugan in case Dugan decided to fire. "Just tell the boys that a storm is coming, to grab their sleeping bags, and we'll walk to the barn and spend the night there."

Maybe it would be better if they were contained. Then Brody and Miles could find them and…then what? Surround the barn? Try to talk Dugan down?

Offer him a way out?

She didn't understand the man's behavior now, but she couldn't chance setting him off by making him mad either. She had to play along until she could delve deeper and figure out a way to convince him to release the children.

Justin cut a frightened look toward Dugan, then stepped over to wake Carlos. The moment Carlos realized what was happening, he glanced at Dugan as if he wanted to kill him.

Carlos had anger issues himself. God, the possibilities of this situation exploding had worsened.

Dugan eased up and pressed the gun to her back again. "Stop wasting time."

"I'm not, but I don't want to upset the kids," she said evenly. Carlos gave her a questioning look, but she forced calm into her voice that belied the fear seeping through her.

"Please help us, Carlos."

His eyes veered across the area toward the woods as if he wanted to run for help but she shot him a warning look. "Just stay calm and do what I say."

He finally nodded, then he and Justin woke the boys one by one. Slowly they roused, all sleepy and confused, but Jordan explained that a storm was brewing so they were going to take shelter in the nearest barn. A couple of the guys protested, but she assured them they would still be camping out.

Then Timmy stirred and saw Dugan, and terror seized his little face.

Jordan stooped to pull him into her arms. "It's okay, Timmy, I'm here."

A guttural sound tore from his throat, and Jordan realized that he recognized Dugan.

MILES REMOVED HIS GUN and checked his pocket for extra ammunition, then circled the front of the Jeep to the driver's side.

Mason folded his arms. "What are you going to do?"

"Kill that SOB."

Mason stepped in front of him, blocking him from getting in the SUV. "Just hold on a damn minute and let's think this through," Mason said. "We have a hostage situation. We should call for backup, at least alert the local sheriff of the situation."

"There's no time."

"What about the other kids on the ranch? If things go bad or if Dugan's accomplice is here, they're in danger, too."

Panic swam in Miles's mind, images of Timmy and Jordan being murdered tormenting him. But Mason was right; there were other kids with Jordan.

Plus all the other campers on the BBL.

Brody raced up in his truck and screeched to a stop. When he climbed out, he looked harried. "I got here as fast as I could. Any more news?"

"We were just discussing a strategy," Mason said.

Brody pulled at his chin. "I called the sheriff and informed him that we have trouble."

Miles threw his hands up in the air. "Dammit, if cops swarm, Dugan may panic and start shooting."

"I'll handle the sheriff," Brody said. "But we need men here to clear the other campers while we deal with the hostage situation."

"We should call in a negotiator," Mason suggested.

"Let me deal with him," Miles said. "I'm the one he wants."

Mason and Brody exchanged worried looks. "I called Wes Lee," Brody said, "but he's not answering his phone. I'm afraid we may have lost him, too."

Miles chewed the inside of his cheek. "I say we ride out to the camp and find out."

Mason quirked his mouth to the side. "We'll need to go in quietly."

Miles nodded. "Let's saddle some horses and ride to the creek on the other side of the campsite. Then we'll move in on foot."

Brody and Mason both agreed. "I'll send Cook with you," Brody offered.

"No, have him help you and the sheriff round up all the other kids and workers and corral them into the dining hall. We can protect them better if they're contained."

Brody adjusted his hat. "Good idea." He stepped onto the porch to phone Cook and wait for the sheriff, and Mason and Miles headed toward the stable.

They saddled horses in record time, then both mounted their rides, their weapons by their sides. Miles knew the ranch layout better and led the way, keeping his eyes peeled for trouble.

Every night sound, crack of a tree limb, coyote's cry made his heart pound harder. It was less than a mile to the west side of the creek, where he brought his horse to a stop and climbed off. Mason followed, the two of them tying their mounts to a nearby post and crossing through the woods, then along the bank until they reached the most shallow part of the creek.

Miles pushed aside a patch of weeds and studied the area, listening for sounds of the kids, for Jordan, anything to verify they were still there and alive.

But it was so dark he could only make out the lingering smoke curling toward the sky from the earlier campfire. He motioned Mason to follow and stay alert, then crept through the woods and started across the creek.

The woods seemed unusually quiet for the danger that he knew waited, alarming him more. And as he pushed through the shallow water and eased onto the embankment, he scanned the area around the fire.

Mason searched the edge of the woods. "I found Haddock. He didn't make it."

Dammit. Miles spotted Wes Lee and hurried over to where he lay in the dirt. He knelt and checked his pulse. "He's still breathing."

Then he searched the campsite. The sleeping bags, the kids…Jordan…they were all gone.

His chest clenched. What in the hell had Dugan done to the boys?

He turned and scanned the thicket of trees. Could he already have killed Jordan and Timmy and left them somewhere out in the woods to die alone?

Chapter Twelve

Miles's head spun. He needed help for Lee, but he also had to find Jordan and Timmy and the other kids.

Mason walked up behind him. "I'll call for an ambulance."

Miles shook his head. "No, let me call Dr. Richmond. He'll get here faster than transporting Lee to the E.R." He called the doc and quickly explained the circumstances.

Mason grabbed a blanket one of the kids left behind, tore it in half, then wadded it up and pressed it against Lee's wound to stem the blood flow.

"I'll be right there," Dr. Richmond said.

"Bring help to move him to the hospital," Miles said. "And do it quietly. The man who shot him is armed and dangerous. He's taken hostages on the ranch. We don't want to send him into a shooting rampage with sirens."

"I understand."

Miles gave him directions to the camp, then turned to Mason. "I'm going to track down the others. Wait here for the doctor."

Mason nodded, then shined a flashlight along the ground and gestured toward the footprints in the dirt. "There's a start."

Miles took the flashlight. "Thanks."

Mason caught his arm before he walked away. "Be careful, McGregor. We want Dugan alive, not to turn this into some vigilante killing."

Miles cursed through his teeth. "He has my little boy."

"I know," Mason said in a low voice. "And when you save Timmy, you don't want to go to prison and leave him on his own. He's lost his mother. He needs his father to raise him."

Emotions flooded Miles. On a rational level, he knew Mason was right. But his rage at the injustice of Dugan's crimes, at the fact he'd gone free, killed Marie and was terrorizing Timmy and Jordan and the other kids with them, heated his blood.

Dammit. He wanted to destroy Dugan.

To see him dead.

Lee groaned and Mason knelt beside him and patted his shoulder. "Help is on the way."

His gaze met Miles's, his earlier warning lingering in the air between them. But Miles didn't have time to debate what he would do if he confronted Dugan.

He couldn't make promises he might not be able to keep.

"They can't have gone far if they're on foot," Miles said.

"True. And I didn't see signs of tire tracks. Although Dugan could have parked somewhere nearby and walked into the camp."

Miles's pulse jumped. If he had a car, he could be off the ranch by now with Timmy and Jordan.

"I need to go," he told Mason. "Once Lee is with the doc, track down Ables."

Miles didn't wait for a response. He turned and waved his flashlight across the ground. Like Mason, he didn't spot tire tracks, only blurred footprints. Several smaller ones, mixed and overlying as if the boys had dragged their feet and walked in a single-file line.

It appeared as if they were heading northeast, back toward the barn about a quarter mile from the camp. That barn was empty now except for bales of hay, and fairly isolated from the rest of camp.

Had Dugan parked near there so he could escape?

He spotted a piece of another blanket caught on a branch, then more footprints. A medium-sized boot print that looked as if it belonged to a woman. Jordan's. They were interspersed between the others. Occasionally he noticed toe drag marks in the dirt.

Jordan had intentionally made the indentations, leaving a bread trail for him to follow.

His admiration for her rose another notch, and he forged on, his heart pounding wildly with every second. A few more feet and he spotted a button, one that looked as if it had come from the shirt Jordan had been wearing before he'd left for the prison.

He sucked in a sharp breath, hoping she'd pulled it off and dropped it as a sign, not that Dugan had done it.

He scanned the area, the bushes and weeds, to make sure Dugan hadn't hurt her and left her to die, but thankfully he didn't find her.

Another few feet and he spotted the barn.

"Dear God, please let them be all right," he whispered.

Then he drew his gun, braced it to fire and headed closer.

"You have to let us go," Jordan said as she gestured for Carlos and Justin to secure the boys against the haystacks. "Miles and Brody are probably already looking for us."

Rory made a whimpering sound, and Malcolm spit into the dirt at Dugan's feet.

Dugan raised his arm to hit the boy, but Jordan stepped in front of him. "So far you haven't hurt any of the children," Jordan said. "Doing that will only make matters worse for you."

Carlos squared his shoulders as if he was a man accustomed to fighting people like Dugan every day. A testament to the hard life he'd lived. "Leave her alone."

Dugan raised his weapon and aimed it at Jordan's face. "If

you don't want anyone hurt, keep them quiet and make sure they don't try to pull anything."

He cut his eyes toward Carlos in warning. Carlos started to step forward as if ready to fight, but Jordan pressed her hand against his chest to stop him. "Stay calm, Carlos. It'll be all right."

She raised her chin a notch. "If you don't want trouble, then put away the gun."

Rory whimpered again, and Justin pulled him over to comfort him. Timmy was staring wide-eyed at Dugan, his body shaking violently.

"Listen, you have me as a hostage," Jordan said, desperate to protect the boys. "The kids will only slow you down, so take me and leave them behind."

"No, Jordan," Carlos pleaded.

"I'm scared," Wayling whispered.

Dugan waved the gun toward the kids who were now huddled in a group, as if sticking together could keep them safe. Both Justin and Carlos had bravely placed themselves in front of the boys as protectors.

These poor kids had seen violence before, but now they showed more courage in the face of danger than anyone she'd ever known.

"Robert," Jordan said, resorting to Dugan's first name to make a personal connection. "I know you must have had a bad childhood yourself." She gestured toward the boys. "Just like these kids. Think about how you felt when you were a little boy."

Pain and a wild kind of fear creased his angular face. "You don't know anything about how I grew up."

She wished she had researched his past, but she hadn't, so she had to make a guess. To assimilate a profile.

His M.O., the fact that he chose women to murder, that they all looked similar, except for Marie, and the fact that he'd called them whores suggested an abusive past. Maybe sexually, definitely emotionally. "I know your mother hurt you. That you wanted her love but that she must not have given it to you."

Fury flared in his eyes. "I told you not to talk about my mother."

"Then tell me about your father," Jordan said calmly. "What was he like?"

"How the hell should I know?" Dugan shouted.

"So you didn't know him?"

"I didn't even know his name," Dugan said. "Hell, my mother didn't know it. But that's not what this is about."

So his mother must have had men. A lot of them.

"Maybe not." She forced herself to soften her tone, to sound sympathetic. "Remember what it was like when you were that little boy. When you were scared and all you wanted was your mother or someone you loved to hold you."

Dugan stared at her for a long minute, his expression so agitated that Jordan feared she'd gone too far. But she had to defuse the situation.

"Think this through." She motioned toward the boys who had quieted but watched her and Dugan. "You want your freedom. There's no way you can escape with these children underfoot. Take me and I'll help you."

Tension thrummed through the air as she waited on his response. He turned and paced across the space, waving the gun at her and the kids, his movements jerky.

Finally he whirled around and aimed the gun at her. "All right, but we're taking the boy."

Jordan shook her head. "No, please leave him. He's innocent—"

"He's McGregor's son." Dugan walked over and snatched Timmy up by the shirt. Timmy released a sob as Dugan dragged him toward her. Jordan caught Timmy against her legs and cradled him against her.

"Shh, honey, it's okay, I'll take care of you."

Dugan pointed the gun at the other boys, then at Jordan's head. "Stay here. If you move, I'll shoot her."

"No!" Wayling and Rory cried.

Justin shielded them with his body while Carlos caught a charging Malcolm by the arm.

"Don't hurt her," Carlos muttered.

Dugan glared at them. "I mean it. If you move, she's dead."

Carlos nodded, then Dugan shoved her and Timmy out the side barn door.

"Where are we going?" Jordan asked.

"Do you ever shut up?" Dugan shouted.

Timmy stumbled, and she grabbed his hand to keep him from falling. Suddenly leaves rustled to the side. Jordan slanted her gaze toward the noise.

Then a figure stepped from the woods, his look lethal. "Dugan, it's over. Let them go."

Miles…thank God he'd found them.

Dugan cursed, shoved her and Timmy back toward the barn, then fired his gun at Miles.

Terror filled Jordan as she and Timmy fell inside the barn, and another gunshot echoed through the air.

Jordan said a silent prayer that he hadn't hit Miles. Poor Timmy needed his father now more than ever.

MILES DUCKED TO THE SIDE just in time to dodge the bullet. Another pinged off a tree near him, and he tried to focus on Dugan. If he just shot the man, he could rescue Timmy and Jordan and the others.

He raised his gun. Dugan was using Jordan and Timmy like a shield, and he couldn't take a chance on hitting one of them. Then Jordan and his son disappeared back inside the barn. For a fraction of a second, he had a view of Dugan.

His hand shook, and he narrowed his eyes, determined to make the shot count. One bullet to the chest, that's all he needed.

Revenge flared hot in his blood, the taste of it so delicious he savored the moment of victory. The sound of the bullet cracking the man's ribs.

He envisioned Dugan falling to the ground, eating dust, his blood running from his body like a stream, gurgling and bubbling as the life drained from the sick man...

Dugan gone...

The violence ending.

His son safe.

But Dugan vaulted inside the barn before he could fire a round.

Dammit.

Cold sweat exploded on his head and body. Had he messed up by showing himself? Would Dugan take it out on Jordan and Timmy and the other kids?

He inhaled a sharp breath, strained to hear what was going on inside, braced himself for another gunshot, for a scream...

Nausea rose to his throat. Surely the man wasn't so sadistic he'd hurt all those innocent boys?

But images of the bodies of the women he'd murdered, of Marie's bloody corpse, flickered across his mind and he knew Dugan was capable of anything. The man had no conscience.

Worse, he was desperate. He'd completely deviated from his pattern and was out of control, acting on instinct and panic with no rational thought as to the fact that his behavior made him look guilty of the crimes he'd been released for.

Still, the accomplice—Ables, he now believed the man to be—was out there.

Mason would alert the authorities and hopefully they would apprehend him. But what kind of damage would he do first?

Was he stalking another victim now? Did he have another woman in his clutches, had he tied her down, raped her, slashed her throat?

A seed of terror seized him, for the first time in months doubts hammering at him.

What if *he* had been wrong all along?

What if Dugan hadn't murdered all four women? What if Ables had? Or perhaps they'd taken turns? Maybe it had been a game and they'd been keeping score?

Had he screwed up and set the wheels in motion to cause Marie's death because he'd missed something? Or what if Belsa had killed her?

Dugan had insisted on his innocence all through the trial. He'd claimed he had been set up.

Was Dugan here to exact revenge because he was innocent—because Miles had been so sure Dugan was guilty that he'd convicted him when the real killer was still hunting?

Chapter Thirteen

Jordan's knees hit the floor of the barn, but she ignored the pain. The boys looked terrified. "It's okay," she said, praying she was right and that Miles hadn't been hit.

She had to be rational. Keep the boys calm. If one of them tried to do something heroic like jump Dugan or escape, it could be dangerous for all of them.

Timmy clung to her. "Go on, sweetie, go sit with Carlos and the others." His big eyes looked terrified and hesitant, but she stroked his hair. "It's all right. Now do as I say."

Carlos held out his hand. "Come on, sport."

Timmy ran over to him, and Carlos pulled him up against the wall beside him.

Meanwhile, Dugan paced by the door, his harried, jerky movements indicating his agitation. He felt trapped. That could be dangerous or work to her advantage if she played him right.

"Dugan, listen to me," Miles shouted from outside.

Relief swam through Jordan. If Miles was talking, he must not be shot. He would rescue them, she knew it.

Dugan inched to the door, cracked it a notch and shouted, "Come any closer and I start shooting in here."

Jordan's breath caught, and the kids made a collective gasp.

"Did you hear me, McGregor?" Dugan made a show of

glancing at her, then the kids. "Let me see, who's going to get the first bullet?"

Jordan moved to block his view of the kids. "You really don't want to do that, Robert."

"I'm putting my gun down," Miles shouted. "But we have to talk, Dugan. You need my help to escape, and it won't work if you hurt one of those kids."

Through the slit in the doorway, Jordan saw Miles inching toward the barn, his hands raised in surrender.

Her heart stalled in her chest. What if Dugan shot him?

"Don't come any further," Dugan warned.

Miles halted, his expression grim. "Come on, Dugan. You want me. Just send the kids out and take me as your hostage."

"No, no, no," Dugan sang. "I'm not falling for your tricks."

Jordan gently laid her hand on his arm. "I know you, Robert, you understand how these boys feel because you were afraid when you were little."

"Stop trying to get into my head," he snarled.

"You know you can't stay here," Jordan said quietly. "And you can't take all these boys with you, so why not let them go? They're only going to be a liability."

He flicked his gaze toward the kids, seemingly contemplating her words.

"You'll still have me," Jordan continued. "You can get a car or a helicopter and we can leave. But you can't run with this group. And if you hurt any of them, it won't even matter if you were innocent or guilty before. The police will just come after you harder."

"McGregor will never stop anyway," Dugan bit out.

"Maybe not. But when you were little, you wanted someone to save you from your home. From whatever hurt you." Despite the fact that he terrified her, she forced herself to stroke his arm in a soothing gesture. "You can do that for these boys. You can save them like you wanted to be saved."

A heartbeat of silence lingered, riddled with tension, with emotions, with fear. Dugan paced, obviously warring with the decision in his mind. Something was off about the way he was acting, but she couldn't put her finger on it.

It was almost as if he'd suffered a psychotic break. Or perhaps he normally took medication and was off of it. His eyes didn't seem to be able to focus, and she noticed a nervous tick in his jaw. It was slight, and something new that hadn't been evident in his TV interviews.

"Dugan," Miles shouted again. "I'm waiting. Send out the kids and I'm yours."

Anger once again heated his eyes, and he swung the gun toward Justin. Wayling and Rory were hovering by him, knees drawn, faces strained.

"The little guy with the red hair, come here."

Jordan's throat clogged with fear, but Rory stood on shaky legs and walked toward her. Jordan grabbed his hand and pulled him against her side. "Don't hurt him, Robert."

That jaw twitched again. Then he poked Rory with the butt of his gun. "Go on, kid, get out of here."

Relief swirled in Jordan's chest, and she nodded toward Rory. Dugan pushed her to the door of the barn and held her in front of him, the gun at her throat.

"One of the kids is on his way out, but if you make a move, the woman gets it in the head," Dugan yelled.

Jordan's pulse pounded as her gaze met Miles's. His look was stony, his big body rigid, the fury radiating from him palpable. She tried to offer him a smile, to let him know that everyone was safe for now, but she wasn't sure she pulled it off.

Her hand fumbled on Rory's arm. "Go on, sweetie. Run outside to Miles."

Rory looked up at her with terrified eyes. But she also saw worry and guilt, as if he hated to leave the others behind. "It'll be all right, I promise," Jordan whispered. "Just go on. We'll join you soon."

She gently nudged him through the door and saw visible relief on Miles's face. Jordan felt the same except there were still five other boys that needed saving.

She prayed she could talk Dugan into releasing all of them. Then she would start fighting for her own life.

MILES'S HEART ACHED as little Rory raced toward him. He had texted Brody their location, and he heard a horse galloping up and glanced back to see Brody heading his way.

He swept Rory up and raced back to the edge of the woods just as Brody slowed the horse to a stop. Brody's grim expression mirrored his own, but the fact that Dugan had released Rory was a good sign.

"What's the situation?" Brody asked as he took Rory from Miles and eased him down behind a massive oak.

"Dugan appeared to be trying to get away with Jordan and Timmy when I arrived, but when he saw me, he shoved them back in the barn." Miles scrubbed his hand down his chin. "Jordan must have convinced him to release Rory. Hopefully he'll let all the kids go."

Although he had a bad feeling he wouldn't release Timmy. Dugan was sadistic. He'd want to hold that bargaining chip over him just to twist the knife deeper in his gut.

He turned to Rory. "Is anyone hurt?"

Rory shook his head no, but his lower lip quivered. "But he gots a gun and a knife and he hitted Miss Jordan."

Miles's chest clenched.

"Is she okay?" Brody asked.

Rory nodded. "She tolded him to keep her and let us go."

Miles pinched the bridge of his nose. Jordan was sacrificing herself to save the boys.

He and Brody exchanged worried looks.

"Stay down," Brody told Rory. "We'll see if we can get your buddies out."

"How's Lee?" Miles asked.

Brody shrugged. "He'll make it. The sheriff and one of his deputies are combing the ranch in case Dugan's accomplice shows up. Another deputy and Cook are standing guard over the campers and employees at the dining hall." Brody tilted his hat back. "Blackpaw said you discovered that Dugan has a half brother who visited him at the prison?"

"Yes. Blackpaw's searching for him."

"Maybe we should call in the feds," Brody suggested.

"There's no time," Miles said. "Let me try to talk Dugan down."

Brody gave him a warning look. "Make sure that's your priority."

Miles ground his teeth. "Of course that's my priority."

Concern flickered in Brody's eyes. "But I know you want Dugan dead. And I understand the reason. If I were in your shoes, I'd probably feel the same way."

Conflicting emotions pummeled Miles. "I do want him dead," he admitted. "But I want Jordan and Timmy and the others out alive. Now trust me to do my job."

Another second passed, then Brody nodded.

Once again Miles erected that steel wall around his emotions. He had to think like a cop, use his skills, get everyone out alive.

Especially Timmy and Jordan.

Hell, he shouldn't think that way. It was selfish, but he couldn't help himself. He loved his son more than his own life.

And he was starting to care for Jordan....

Yes, he'd save them. But he'd save the others, too.

Then he'd deal with Dugan and Ables and find out the truth about the murders so he could make the culprits pay.

"THANK YOU FOR LETTING Rory go, Robert," Jordan said. "That was the right thing to do."

Dugan raked his hand through his neatly manicured hair, spiking the ends in disarray, then pushed his face into hers. "Don't sound so condescending. I still have the power here."

"I know you do," Jordan said, striving for calm. "And you also know that these kids will only slow you down when it's time for you to leave. So why not send them outside now?"

He twisted around, stared at the children, cursed, then paced back and forth. His hand was shaking, his jaw twitching, his body jerking erratically. He was losing control and she didn't know when his fuse might blow.

"Please," Jordan said softly. "You'll still have me. That's all you need."

His hiss echoed in the silence while Justin and Carlos did their best to keep the boys quiet. Timmy had drawn his knees to his chest and buried his head against them as if he had to shut out the world.

Dugan pointed to Malcolm and Justin. "All right, you two." He yanked Malcolm by the arm and held the gun at his back. "Don't try anything, big guy, or your friend gets it."

Malcolm made a gallant attempt to hide his fear, but Jordan saw his body tremble. Justin frowned up at Dugan. "You big bullies are all the same."

"You got nerve, kid," Dugan bellowed.

Justin looked as if he intended to say more; Jordan remembered his story. He had not only been bullied as a kid, but he'd been beaten by his stepfather. The stepfather was arrested only after putting Justin in the hospital twice. Finally his mother left the man, but the mental scars remained. Kids who grew up with abusive parents learned early on how to avoid inciting their wrath.

Either that, or they rebelled when they were older and turned violent themselves. Justin had traveled that path but had come back. Still, Dugan must be pushing his buttons, just as he was doing with Carlos and Malcolm.

"Justin," she said with a warning note in her voice. "Please take Malcolm outside."

Dugan jabbed Justin. "You think you're tough, kid."

Jordan squeezed Justin's arm. They couldn't risk antagonizing the man.

Justin released a shaky breath. "No, sir."

Dugan twisted his mouth from side to side as if in indecision, but finally motioned toward the door with a wave of the gun. "Go now or you lose your chance."

Jordan stepped to the door. "Miles, Justin and Malcolm are coming out now."

Miles emerged from the woods and walked toward them, but Dugan shouted at him to stop. Seconds later, Justin took Malcolm's arm and the two of them hurried toward Miles. He swept them to safety behind some trees with Rory.

"Thank you, Dugan," Miles yelled as he stepped back into the clearing, his hands once again splayed as if in surrender. "Now release Jordan and the other boys and I'm all yours."

"You don't get it, do you?" Dugan yelled back. "You ruined my life. I intend to do the same to yours."

"You've already done that," Miles said. "You killed Timmy's mother and terrified him."

"Stop this madness," Jordan said behind Dugan. "Let the boys go and prove you aren't the monster Miles accused you of being."

Dugan cursed, rammed his hand against the wall with a bang, then swung the gun toward Carlos and Wayling. Timmy jerked his head up and whimpered. Jordan wanted to go to him, but any sudden movement might set Dugan off, so she remained still, calm, focused.

"You two, get up," Dugan said. He shoved the gun in

Carlos's face and jerked Wayling's arm. Wayling grunted in pain, but Carlos simply stared Dugan in the eyes.

These boys had already seen too much violence in their lives. They shouldn't be so hardened, but at this moment, she was glad they were tough enough to realize that reacting might make things worse.

Carlos gripped Wayling by the shirt collar. "Come on, kid. Let's get out of here." He glanced back at Jordan before he stepped outside. "Will you be okay?"

She forced a smile. "Yes, just take Wayling and be there for the other boys. They need you, Carlos."

A moment of understanding, and pride flickered in his eyes, and Jordan's heart squeezed. When they ended this situation safely, she would commend all these boys on their bravery.

Miles stepped out to usher Carlos and Wayling to join the others with Brody, then he returned midway again. "Now, Dugan, send Timmy and Jordan out and I'll give you whatever you want."

Jordan sucked in a sharp breath. Judging from the maniacal look in Dugan's eyes, he wanted Miles dead.

And she couldn't live with that.

"Make the deal," Jordan said. "Miles can arrange transportation for you. Then you'll be free. That's what you want, not to hurt an innocent child like you were once."

Dugan swung around as if to hit her, and Timmy made a noise then rocked himself back and forth.

For a moment, Dugan seemed mesmerized by his behavior as if it touched some distant memory chord. Then he moved back to the barn door and nudged his gun into the opening.

"All right, McGregor. Get me a helicopter cleared to take off and cross into Mexico, then I'll let the kid and your lover girl go."

Jordan held her breath.

Miles shouted back, "I'll have one here in an hour. Now send out my son."

"No way," Dugan said with a bitter laugh. "Get the chopper first. And I want clearance to get to Mexico without cops on my tail."

"All right," Miles agreed. "But you have to release Timmy and Jordan first. You can take me instead."

"Fine," Dugan said, although Jordan saw the twisted look in his eyes and knew he was lying.

Which meant she had to keep hacking away at him. Find out why he wanted to go to Mexico. If there was someone he was running to.

"One hour," Dugan shouted back to Miles. "Not another minute longer." He jerked Jordan up to the doorway and pointed the gun to her temple. "And if I see any cops or hear anyone approaching, she takes a bullet in the head, and you'll never see your son alive again."

Jordan reached up to touch Dugan. "Please, think about Timmy. Hurting him is senseless."

Irrational anger flared in his eyes as he swung his hand back and sent her sailing against the wall. Her head hit the edge, blood trickled into her eyes.

Timmy jumped up and suddenly screamed, "Stop!"

Jordan swayed and reached for him, but Timmy threw himself at Dugan, beating at his legs with his fists.

Dugan grabbed Timmy and flung him off of him, so hard he stumbled and hit the floor. Jordan jumped up to protect him and slammed her weight into Dugan.

The gun went off.

The shot echoed in the air, and pain sliced through her, the world spinning as she fell to the floor.

RED DOTS SPLATTERED the air in front of Timmy's eyes. The scream started inside his head, loud and shrill, over and over.

He couldn't stand it. Couldn't stop it.

He closed his eyes and covered his ears. He had to stop the noise.

But he could still hear her. His mommy. Crying. Screaming.

The red...it covered everything. His mommy's neck. Her body. The floor...

And now it was all over Jordan....

No...she couldn't die and leave him like his mommy had....

He had to stop her from dying. Had to stop the bad man.

He opened his eyes and blinked. The red...there it was again. Jordan on the floor. The man over her.

He jumped up and ran toward him again. This time he would make him stop. He had to.

It was his fault his mama died.

It would be his fault if Jordan did, too....

Chapter Fourteen

Miles normally didn't flinch at the sound of a gunshot, but this one nearly brought him to his knees. He heaved for a breath, grabbed his gun and started to run forward but Brody called his name.

"Wait," Brody said in a low voice.

"No, Timmy or Jordan might be hit." *Dear God, please don't let them be dead.*

A commotion sounded from inside the barn, and Miles froze. "Jordan?" A pained silence tore at his gut, making him desperate to see what was going on. "Dugan, what happened? Is someone hurt?"

"Shut up!" Dugan suddenly appeared at the barn door, his face barely visible behind the wooden doorway he was using as a barrier. "You promised me a chopper, now where is it?"

"Our deal was that you let Jordan and Timmy go and then I give you a way out," Miles shouted, unable to control his anger. "Are Jordan and Timmy okay?"

By God, if Dugan had hurt one of them, he would die.

A slow and painful death.

"Your son is fine," Dugan said.

Relief made Miles dizzy. Then again, the sicko could be lying. "What about Jordan?"

A long pause, then a raspy reply. "She's alive."

Miles glanced back at Brody and saw the boys fidgeting

nervously, whispering in hushed tones, their faces drawn with worry and anger.

"I need proof," Miles said.

A bitter laugh echoed from Dugan. "Do what I said or you won't ever see them."

"Not working this time," Miles said, standing his ground. "How do I know you didn't shoot both of them?"

A string of curses rolled off Dugan's tongue. Gone was the smooth-talking, confident man in the courtroom who had won half the jurors over and played innocent until even Miles had momentarily wondered if he had arrested the wrong man.

This was a desperate man out for revenge, one who had been cornered and saw no way out.

The most dangerous kind...

Still now, with Ables on the loose, he had to wonder if Dugan had committed all the murders or if they'd worked together as he'd suspected. Or could Ables have committed the crimes alone?

Another possibility nagged at him.

What if the half brothers had some bad history and Ables had set Dugan up to take the fall?

No...otherwise Dugan wouldn't be here now...unless he wanted a hostage to help him until he could get to Ables. Maybe Ables was in Mexico....

"Let me see them or no chopper," Miles said more firmly.

Another hiss echoed from the barn, then a moan, and suddenly Dugan shoved Timmy in the doorway. He held his son by the collar, the gun to his head, an evil leer on his face.

Miles choked back the bile clogging his throat. Timmy was so close...yet so far away. He wanted to touch him, to yank him away from this monster. But any sudden move could mean death for him and Jordan. "Are you okay, son?"

For the first time since Marie's death, Timmy actually

looked at him. Tears blurred his eyes, but he gave a small nod. Miles's heart broke.

"What about Jordan?" he asked, his breath stalling in his chest.

"You saw the boy, now I want to see that chopper," Dugan said.

Then he disappeared back inside the barn with Timmy, leaving Miles to wonder if Jordan was alive or if he'd killed her.

JORDAN FOUGHT A WAVE of dizziness as she pushed herself up from the floor to a sitting position. Near the barn door Timmy was sobbing softly as Dugan held him by the collar. She wanted to go to him, but she couldn't chance spooking Dugan.

Pain ricocheted through her shoulder where the bullet had struck, and she pressed her hand to the wound to stop the blood flow. Her hand felt sticky and damp, but she wasn't bleeding badly. Maybe just a flesh wound...

Timmy tried to twist away from the man and she called his name. "Timmy, it's okay, sweetie. I'm all right."

Dugan spun around and glared at her, then slammed the barn door shut and shoved Timmy. He ran to her and collapsed at her side. She cradled him next to her.

"It's going to be all right."

"B...ut y...ou're hurt," Timmy said with big eyes.

They'd waited so long to hear Timmy speak again, and now he was worried about her. Tears blurred her eyes, but she blinked them away.

"It's not bad," she said gently. "I'm going to be fine and so are you."

Dugan paced again, his agitation obvious with his jumpy movements. "I know you didn't mean to hurt me," Jordan said, determined to calm him. "It was an accident. I'll tell them that when the police come."

"You're a fool, lady," Dugan said. "The police…Mc-Gregor…no one is going to lock me up again."

He wanted to go to Mexico. Again, she wondered if someone was waiting on him there.

Timmy quieted beside her, and she wrapped her arm around him and held him close. He had tried to protect her. Poor little guy. Had Dugan's attack on her triggered memories of his attack on Marie?

"There must be someone you want to see now you're free," Jordan said.

"Free?" Dugan growled. "I won't be free till I get rid of McGregor."

Timmy shuddered next to her, but she stroked his arm. "I don't understand why you came after him and why you killed his wife," Jordan said. "You were out of jail. All you had to do was walk away."

Dugan's face twisted into a nasty grimace. "Walk away? McGregor ruined my reputation, my name. He convinced everyone I was guilty."

"But the courts freed you."

"Do you think that changed the way people looked at me?" He waved the gun wildly. "Janet even left me."

"Janet?"

"Yeah, the only woman I ever loved believed him over me," he said bitterly. "I've lost everything."

He was delusional, still not able to confess that he was a murderer. Her best strategy would be to play along. Feed his ego.

The mind was like a puzzle—if she could figure out where the pieces went, she could complete the picture.

That would help her know how to deal with him…to reach him.

"So far you haven't hurt anyone here," Jordan said. "And

Miles believes there's a copycat, that someone else killed those women. Maybe someone who wanted to set you up."

A fire lit Dugan's eyes. "Yes, yes, that's what happened. I told them that over and over and over."

Jordan nodded. "I think he's on the man's track now."

Hope warred with the anger in Dugan's eyes. "You're lying."

"No, I'm not. Miles knows you didn't kill June Kelly. That made him start thinking that maybe you were innocent all along. That this other man committed the murders and framed you."

"He thinks that?" Dugan's voice trembled.

Jordan nodded again. "But holding us hostage only makes you look guilty."

He was, of course, for killing Haddock. And Lee…she had no idea if he'd survived.

"Just let us go, and take that helicopter. You can leave, meet that woman you love and explain that we were wrong. Then the two of you can build a life together in Mexico."

"Yes, Mexico," Dugan said. "I have to go to Mexico."

Jordan continued to stroke Timmy's hair. He had finally stopped crying and looked stronger now, as if speaking had relinquished some of his fear. She only hoped that he could fully recover once this nightmare ended.

"Why Mexico?" Jordan asked, resorting to the calming voice she used with patients.

A muscle ticked in his jaw. "Anybody ever tell you that you ask too many questions?"

Jordan shrugged. "I'm a woman, we like to talk. I know Mexico is beautiful, but is there another reason? Do you have friends or family there?"

He had reacted when she'd talked about his mother.

"Is that where your mother lives?" she asked.

An odd expression colored his face, and he walked the

length of the barn, then paused and leaned back against the wall as if remembering something.

"Did you grow up there?" she asked. "Or maybe your mother took you on vacation."

A bitter laugh that sounded far away echoed in the air. "My mama didn't have money for vacations. She used every penny she made on cigarettes, booze and drugs."

Another piece of the puzzle. His mother had slept around—or was a prostitute. Had she made him watch?

If so, no wonder he hated women and thought they were whores.

The fact he'd grown up without money had motivated him to work hard and become financially independent.

Suddenly Miles shouted again. "Dugan, the chopper is on its way. Is Jordan all right?"

"I'm—" Jordan opened her mouth to shout, but Dugan backhanded her. Her head whipped sideways. Timmy jumped up to defend her, but she grabbed him and held him firmly by her side.

Dugan checked his watch. "Five minutes, that's all you have left," he yelled. "Five minutes till I start shooting."

Jordan gritted her teeth. She had to keep talking. Keep him thinking, distracted.

"It is your mother you're going to see in Mexico, isn't it?" she asked.

He stormed toward her, lifted her chin and pierced her with his maniac eyes. "Yes. Don't you think she'll be proud of what her baby boy has become?"

A cold chill slithered up Jordan's spine. Now she understood. All the women he had killed—they were only substitutes for the mother who had sold her body to support her habits.

He was going to end his killing spree. But he intended to do it by finally murdering the real source of his anger and hatred—his mother.

MILES WANTED TO HEAR from Jordan. He told himself she had to be okay, that he had heard her voice just then, although he couldn't be sure.

"Where are we on the chopper, Brody?" Miles asked.

Brody cleared his throat. "Johnny said it would be here in a few minutes. We have to keep Dugan calm."

Miles nodded. His son's life depended on it.

"I talked to the sheriff. I'm moving these kids to the dining hall with the others."

"Good. We don't want them out in the open in case something goes wrong." And bullets started flying. "Any word from Cook? Have they spotted Ables on the ranch?"

Brody shook his head. "Hopefully that's a good sign."

"Maybe. But he still could be hiding out, waiting to help Dugan escape."

"We'll keep looking," Brody said. "The sheriff called in a couple more deputies to comb the property. One of them is close by." He pointed to the rocks on the hill to the north. "He's watching from that angle in case we need him. And when Dugan heads to the chopper, we'll catch him. Or the deputy might get a shot at him."

Miles clenched his jaw and stepped behind the tree near the boys. "No one shoots unless I say so. We can't do anything to endanger Timmy or Jordan."

Brody nodded, then gestured toward the group of boys. "My truck is about two hundred feet away, hidden behind some mesquites. I'm going to drive you back to the dining hall."

Carlos stood and faced Miles and Brody. "I want to stay here and make sure Miss Jordan and Timmy are okay."

"Me, too," Justin said.

The other boys all jumped up to join Carlos and Justin as if they were a team.

These kids all had troubled pasts, and the fact that they were bound together now by this event had seemed to strengthen them. Still, it was his job to protect them.

"I know you guys are worried, but you have to go with Brody."

Carlos crossed his arms. "We're not kids so don't treat us that way."

Miles laid his hand on the teenager's shoulder. "I realize that, Carlos, and you've been a tremendous asset here. But it's time for the lawmen to handle it. You can help by protecting the younger kids."

Carlos squared his shoulders and stared into his eyes as if he wanted to argue. Miles knew he was trying to be a man, and felt for the kid. So many of these boys had seen things no kid should have seen.

Just like his son.

They'd had to grow up fast.

Miles pulled him aside for a moment while Brody talked to the others. "Please," Miles said. "Help me out, Carlos. The other guys look up to you. You're their leader." He gestured toward the mound of rocks on the hill. "The deputy is waiting on that hill, the chopper is on its way, but we have no idea if things will get ugly. Dugan is armed and dangerous. We have to get these other boys out of the way in case we have to rush in and rescue Jordan and Timmy. The others will listen to you, so do your job and let me do mine."

Carlos shifted restlessly, then seemed to accept what he'd said. "All right, man. But...don't let anything happen to Miss Jordan. She stood up for all of us in there." He jammed his hands in the pockets of his dusty jeans. "She's getting to him, too."

Miles drew a deep breath. Jordan was smart. She would do that, try to figure out a way to calm him.

He just hoped that it worked and that she and Timmy both came out alive.

DUGAN HAD TO GET THE damn woman out of his head. Stop her incessant talking.

His mind raced, voices whispering at him to shut her up. To torture her and carve her up like the others.

"Just look at Timmy," she said. "Don't you see yourself in him, Robert? Don't you see that innocent little boy? He's lost his mother. All he wants now is to be with some friends. Learn to ride horses and grow up."

"Shut the hell up!" He strode over and slapped her again.

Her head whipped back, and Timmy cried out. Then suddenly the brat ran over and bit his arm.

Dugan bellowed and shook him free, then threw the kid against the hay. Jordan jumped up in front of Timmy, and Dugan shoved her aside. The gun went off again, and Jordan screamed.

"Kill her," the voice whispered. "Take the boy and run. You know what you have to do." Yes, he did. There would be no time for pleasure with her.

Although that certainly would have tormented McGregor more.

He had to get out of here, had to get away.

See his mama.

"Dugan!" Miles shouted.

Outside, footsteps pounded. Something banged against the barn door. Suddenly the side door flew open, and a deputy dived in firing.

Jordan screamed again, and he hit her with the butt of his gun and knocked her to the ground. Timmy dived on top of her.

"Miss Jordan..."

Everything happened so fast. Bullets flying. The deputy shouting his name. McGregor racing in.

Dugan jerked Timmy up and pulled him in front of himself.

McGregor halted and threw his hand up to warn the deputy not to come closer.

Dugan had no choice. The damn bitch started this. But he had to finish it.

He pressed the gun barrel to the boy's head then glared at McGregor. "Don't come any closer or you'll be putting your boy in the ground beside his mother."

Chapter Fifteen

Miles stared at the scene in front of him in horror. Jordan on the ground. Blood on her blouse. Not moving.

Timmy in the clutches of the sadistic monster who'd killed his mother.

Dammit, what had gone wrong? The gunshot…the deputy barging in…

"Daddy?"

Timmy's choked voice dragged Miles back to the moment—his son had actually spoken.

"It's okay, bud. I'm right here." He cleared his throat of the emotions threatening to consume him. "Don't hurt him, Dugan."

"Then stay back." Dugan's hand trembled, which made Miles even more nervous. "Is that chopper outside?"

Miles forced himself to rein in his temper. "Not yet but it's on its way."

The deputy groaned and panic flared in Dugan's eyes. "Where's your car, Deputy?"

Miles glanced at the deputy who was pressing his hand over his thigh to stem the blood flow. "On the hill out back."

"Keys?" Dugan asked.

The deputy dangled them.

"Toss them to me," Dugan ordered.

Timmy struggled but Dugan tightened his grip. "Be still, kid, or your dad will get it."

His harshly spoken words froze Timmy with fear.

Miles silently cursed but gestured for the deputy to toss Dugan the keys. They jangled then fell at Dugan's feet. He stooped down and stuffed them in his pocket.

Miles had to reason with him. "Come on, Dugan, you can get away faster if you're by yourself. Everyone will be looking for you if you kidnap a child."

"Yeah, but no one will shoot." The glow of victory lit Dugan's eyes.

Miles took a step forward. "Taking me hostage serves the same purpose." He rested his hand on the handcuffs at his belt. "Come on, let Timmy go and you can handcuff me."

He'd trade his life for his little boy's any day.

Dugan's mouth crinkled with a smile as he looked down at Timmy. His expression was twisted and demonic.

Then, for a moment, almost affectionate.

What the hell... The sick bastard.

"Sorry, McGregor, but the kid is my best chance." He rubbed one hand over Timmy's head. "Besides, your girlfriend made me start thinking about things. How I never had a kid of my own. How I could have done better than my mother."

Miles's blood ran cold. What was he going to do? Kill him then raise Timmy as his own?

JORDAN SHOOK THE REMNANTS of fog from her mind as she stirred. Her brain felt fuzzy, her temple was throbbing, her arm burning. What had happened?

She heard voices and looked up to see Dugan holding Timmy at gunpoint. Miles was trying to talk him down. The deputy lay injured across from her.

Then Dugan started backing toward the barn door with Timmy as a shield.

"Dugan, don't." Miles lurched forward, but Dugan raised his gun to fire. Jordan had to do something. She couldn't let him kill Miles.

Especially in front of his son.

Summoning all the strength she possessed, she shoved herself up and threw her body at Dugan, knocking the gun upward so it discharged into the air. Timmy yelped, Miles ducked, and the bullet pinged off the roof. Dugan swung his hand back and pushed Jordan back again, then dragged Timmy out the door.

"Stop!" Miles yelled.

But Dugan fired again, and they were helpless to do anything but watch him drag the little boy up the hill toward the woods. Jordan staggered to the door while Miles inched outside, raising his gun and following Dugan.

Seconds later, an engine cut through the night, and she sagged against the doorway as Miles's bellow of frustration echoed through the air.

Jordan ran toward him. Miles looked crazed and swung around to her in a blind panic. "I have to go. Are you all right?"

"Yes, I'll go with you."

"No." Miles touched her head and came away with bloody fingers, then gestured toward her shoulder. "You need a doctor. I'll call an ambulance for you and the deputy while I drive."

Jordan caught his arm. "Please, Miles. I connected with Dugan. I might be able to help."

His gaze latched with hers for a brief moment, then he nodded, took her hand and they raced to his Jeep. She jumped in the passenger side and he tossed her his phone while he peeled down the road after Dugan.

Jordan called Brody and got him on the line "The deputy is alive but was shot in the leg," Jordan said. "Miles and I are chasing Dugan now. He's headed east off the ranch in the deputy's car." Which would make it harder to pinpoint and stop. But hopefully the sheriff was alerting other authorities that he was in a stolen police vehicle.

"I'll call Johnny and tell him to use his chopper and see if he can spot him from the air."

The police siren wailed as his taillights disappeared over the hill. Miles pressed the accelerator, engine redlining as he swerved off the road and took a shortcut across the land.

"We'll catch him," Jordan said, more to reassure herself than him.

He snapped his eyes toward her. "Are you really okay? You look like hell."

"Thanks," Jordan said sarcastically.

His jaw tightened even more if that were possible. "I mean it. You have a head injury and you've been shot. I should be driving you to the emergency room."

"My head is fine. It's just a scratch." She barely resisted rubbing her shoulder. She thought it was just a graze, but the wound stung like fire and a dull ache had rolled through her arm.

Pain underscored his tone. "It damn well better be."

"I'm tougher than I look," she said, desperate to lighten his guilt. For God's sake, he had enough to worry about without being concerned for her.

The Jeep bounced over the ruts and grooves in the terrain, jolting her as he steered it onto the main road from the ranch toward town.

"You certainly are," Miles said, although this time a note of admiration softened his voice. Then he reached out and squeezed her hand. "You nearly got killed trying to protect Timmy."

"We are not going to lose him," Jordan said, injecting confidence into her voice. "We will get him back, Miles." She pointed to the right where Dugan was making a turn.

Miles sped up, skimming the edge of the road and nearly spinning out as he tried to keep up. They chased and followed him for half an hour, twisting onto side roads, veering down alleys in the small town they passed through, driving through the desolate area near the reservation, but when he made it onto the highway toward Mexico, he sped up and maneuvered around traffic.

Minutes later, just as the first rays of sun broke through the night, Dugan disappeared out of sight.

Miles raced across the intersection, tires screeching as a truck roared toward them head-on. The Jeep spun a hundred and eighty degrees, skidded through the traffic light, scraping the side of a parked car along the edge, then careened toward oncoming traffic.

Jordan gripped the dashboard with white knuckles. If Miles didn't get the car under control, they were going to collide.

MILES JERKED THE JEEP to the right, steering into the skid, trying to regain control. Tires squealed, brakes locked, and the wheels screeched as he rode the embankment.

The truck flew toward them, full speed, the thick fog blurring the driver's vision.

Miles swerved again, skimmed the side rail and barreled around a sedan, then swung toward the exit. Free and clear, he skidded to a stop on the side of the road.

He slammed his fist on the steering wheel with a curse. "Dammit, we lost him."

Jordan sighed with relief, her hand still clenching the dash. "Maybe the police will spot him."

"I'll call Johnny. The chopper is our best chance." Miles punched in Johnny's number, praying he was on Dugan's tail. "I lost him," Miles said. "Where are you?"

"I'm flying over the highway, but it's so foggy I can't see a damn thing."

"I'll phone the sheriff and see if they're tailing him." Miles's stomach churned. They had to find him. He couldn't lose Timmy.

When he hung up, Jordan was watching him. She looked pale, her face bruised from the blows Dugan had inflicted. Dried blood still dotted her forehead and hair, and she was gripping her arm at an odd angle.

"What do we do now?" Jordan asked.

Flashes of his son haunted him. Timmy's scared face. His mother's dead body.

Dugan holding the gun to Timmy's head.

He fought through the blaze of panic paralyzing him and forced himself to think like a cop. "There's no need to just drive around. We'll go back to the ranch, pick up our passports and take care of your injuries."

Jordan touched his arm. "Miles, we don't have to take the time to do that."

Miles grunted. "What else can we do now?"

A pained silence fell between them.

"Maybe the police are on him," Jordan said.

Her calm voice snapped him from the overwhelming terror holding him prisoner, and he nodded, then dialed the sheriff's number.

A pause while he waited on the sheriff to pick up. "Sheriff, it's Detective McGregor. We lost Dugan. Have any of your men spotted him?"

"No, but I've put out a statewide alert for him and the deputy's car."

"And an Amber Alert?" Miles asked.

"Yes, I've already put it on the news, but if you have a picture of the boy I'll get that out, too."

Miles started the engine and turned the car back toward

the ranch. "I'm on my way there now. Ask Brody and he can give you one of the pictures from the camp. They took photographs the first day."

"I'm on it," the sheriff said.

"Thanks, Sheriff, I have to go."

He disconnected the call, then turned to Jordan. "Did Dugan tell you where he might be headed?"

"Not exactly." Jordan pursed her lips. "We talked about his family. He kept saying you ruined his life, that everyone believed he was guilty, even the woman he loved."

"The only woman we know about is Renee Balwinger, the one who gave him an alibi, but she's dead."

Jordan shook her head. "I think there's someone else he was involved with. Maybe back before the murders and trial. Her first name was Janet."

Miles's pulse jumped. "Did he mention a last name?"

"No," Jordan said. "But perhaps she attended the trial. There would be records. Or maybe she visited him in prison."

"I'll ask Blackpaw to look into it." Miles sped up, anxious now to reach the ranch. "What else did he say?"

Jordan leaned her head back against the headrest. She looked exhausted and scared, but he knew she wouldn't give up. "I think his mother lives in Mexico, too."

Miles raised a brow. "So he's going to see her?"

"It's possible." Jordan twisted her hands together. "Judging from our conversation, he was abused. And she might have been a prostitute."

Miles sucked in a sharp breath.

"That abuse triggered his hatred of women. He kept referring to his victims as whores."

"He's killing women who look like his mother."

Jordan glanced his way, her eyes glinting with worry. "Yes. Because she's the one he really wanted to kill all along."

Hell. "So he's going to Mexico now to finally make her pay."

Jordan nodded again, resignation in her eyes this time.

Miles accelerated. God. Poor Timmy. He'd already witnessed one murder, and now…would Dugan force him to watch another?

And when he was finished with his mother, what would he do with Timmy?

TIMMY HUGGED THE DOOR. He wanted to get out. Open the door and jump. But he was too scared. If he did, he might get runned over by the other cars. Or the mean man might shoot him.

He was going so fast the tires made noises. The car bumped over rocks and swerved. The man said dirty words and went faster.

Timmy hated him 'cause he hurted Miss Jordan.

Was he the monster that hurted his mommy, too?

He wished he could remember. Then he'd tell on him.

He needed his daddy. His daddy was a good guy. He was a cop. Maybe he'd catch him and put him in jail.

He closed his eyes. Tried to think back.

The red came in splatters. Big puddles. Splashes on the wall. On the floor.

His mommy's face…

He tried to make it go away. To see something else. The monster's face. But it was dark and the black came then.

He rolled his hands into fists. He had to think of a way to get out. To get back to his daddy.

He was mad at him that day his mommy went away. He remembered that. But his daddy had been nice since he brought him to the ranch. And he liked Miss Jordan.

And the horses.

He wanted to go back there now.

Tears burned his eyes, but he scrubbed them away with the backs of his hands. He wasn't no crybaby, not anymore. He wanted to be big and strong like Carlos.

And his daddy.

They would find him. They had to.

But what if they didn't?

He looked up at the mean man. He had weird eyes. And he was saying more dirty words.

"Don't worry, kid," the man said. "We're going to Mexico and no one will ever find us."

Timmy bit his lip to keep from crying. That was what he was afraid of.

Chapter Sixteen

Miles phoned Blackpaw as he drove back to the ranch. "Have you located Ables?"

"No, but I have an address for him and I'm en route there as we speak."

"Good." He explained Jordan's theory about Dugan's former girlfriend and his mother. "I know you're busy, Mason. But I'm wondering if this Janet woman might have been in the courthouse during Dugan's trial. I would call the lieutenant but—"

"You're supposed to be off the case. I'll fill him in on what's happened, then have him fax you a list of the people who attended the trial along with a list of the visitors at the prison. Maybe there will be a crossover."

"Thanks. I have a feeling he might pay her a visit before he goes to his mother's."

"I'll get back to you ASAP."

"Thanks." Miles disconnected the call, turned down the road leading onto the ranch, then drove to the dining hall. "Wait in the Jeep," he told Jordan. "I'm going to check in with Brody then take you home to clean up and check that wound."

Jordan nodded, and he jumped out and rushed in to check on the kids. Brody met him at the door.

"Everyone okay?"

"Yeah. The boys are agitated, but they understand and are worried about Timmy."

"No sightings of Able or any other trouble?"

Brody shook his head. "No. The coroner took Haddock's body, and Lee and the deputy are at the hospital. I called a couple guys I know who work extra security and they're coming over to watch the ranch."

"That's probably wise."

"We're going to feed the kids breakfast, then take them out for a while to work with the horses. But we'll keep them contained within the same area for safety's sake."

Miles nodded. "I'm carrying Jordan back to clean her wounds. I'll keep you posted."

When Miles returned to the Jeep, Jordan's eyes were closed. She looked exhausted, and he still hadn't seen how badly the bullet had grazed her.

She stirred slightly, but kept her eyes closed as he drove to her cabin. When he parked, she jerked awake and climbed out before he could go around to help her.

Anxiety knotted Miles's body as they walked to the door, his hand automatically checking his phone in case he missed a call. Where was Dugan now?

What was he going to do to Timmy?

His stomach heaved. He knew Timmy was terrified, but was he hurt?

Jordan unlocked the door, and he followed her inside, his instincts urging him to turn around and leave.

He should be out there searching for his son. Tracking down Dugan. Saving his little boy.

Jordan must have seen the terror in his eyes because she lifted her hand and pressed it to his jaw. The tender gesture triggered something inside him, a dam of emotions that threatened to erupt.

"I know you're worried," Jordan said. "So am I."

"I was supposed to protect him and I failed," Miles said, his throat aching.

"You did everything you could," she said softly. "And it's not over, Miles. We will find him."

Fear clogged Miles's throat. "But what if it's too late?"

Jordan released a pent-up breath. "You can't think like that. I was getting into Dugan's head, forming a connection."

"What do you mean? He's a sociopath. He has no conscience."

"He was traumatized as a boy. That abuse triggered his behavior." Jordan thumbed his hair back from his forehead. "I don't think he'll hurt Timmy, Miles. I reminded him what it felt like to be a scared little boy. How he felt."

"How can you be sure?"

"I can't," Jordan said. "But I have to believe he'll remember that. That his beef is with his mother, not Timmy."

Miles wanted to believe her so badly his head throbbed. He had to grasp on to the hope she offered. He couldn't survive if he thought Timmy was gone.

Desperate for hope, for some comfort, he reached for Jordan. A heated moment stretched between them as his gaze met hers.

Then a look of hunger and need flared in her eyes. A look that mirrored the feelings raging through him.

He couldn't help himself. He was terrified, hurting… He just wanted to hold her for a minute and absorb her strength.

So he pulled her in his arms and closed his mouth over hers.

JORDAN OPENED HER MOUTH, welcoming Miles's kiss, her need driving her to thread her fingers in his hair and draw him closer. One kiss led to another, their frenzied hunger making her yearn for more.

He deepened the kiss, ran his fingers along her jaw,

dropped tongue lashes along her earlobe and neck until she shivered and rubbed herself against him.

Miles groaned, then cupped her buttocks with his hand and walked her backward until she was pressed against the wall.

His mouth left hers to suckle at her neck, one hand trailing over her shoulder and tugging at her blouse. But the moment he flicked the top button open and saw the blood, he halted.

His gaze met hers, dark, fiercely protective, angry.

"I'm sorry, this is wrong."

"No." She caught his arm before he could pull away. "It's not wrong for two people to comfort each other."

His mouth tightened into a grim line. "You've been injured," he said. "And I need to be looking for my son."

"Miles—"

He traced a finger along the cut on her forehead, his frown deepening. "You probably need stitches or you might scar."

"I don't care about a scar," she said. "I care about you and Timmy."

Pain creased his face. "Jordan…" He closed his eyes. When he opened them, a resolve had set in. "Come on, let's check out your shoulder."

He gently peeled back her blouse, studied the tissue where the bullet had burned the top of her skin, his expression tormented. "I'm sorry you got caught up in this, that you were hurt because of me."

"I'm just glad I was there with Timmy." Jordan kissed his cheek gently. "And I'll be there to help him when we bring him back."

A seed of hope flared in his eyes. His phone beeped that he had a text, and he jerked up to check it.

"What is it?" Jordan asked.

"Blackpaw. The roster for Dugan's trial and the prison visitor list is being faxed to the main house right now. It could be the lead to this woman you mentioned."

"Go pick it up while I shower," Jordan said.

He shook his head. "I don't want to leave you—"

Jordan squeezed his arm. "I'll be fine. The police are looking for Dugan. Brody has security and that other deputy watching for Ables."

Miles wavered slightly, then gave a clipped nod. "Lock the door. I'll be back in a few minutes."

As soon as he left, Jordan hurried into the bathroom. She stripped and examined her injury in the mirror. It was just a graze, but the memory of Dugan holding her, threatening Timmy flashed back and she began to shake all over.

Delayed reaction. She knew the term for it. Understood that now the immediate danger was over, her adrenaline was waning.

She flipped on the shower water and stepped inside. Only the danger wasn't over. Timmy was still with Dugan.

She prayed that she was right and that he wouldn't hurt him.

But the truth was—Robert Dugan was a sociopath. Something had triggered his desperation, incited him to deviate from his pattern, to escalate into taking hostages and risking capture by coming on the ranch.

At this point, he had nothing to lose.

Which meant he might do absolutely anything.

Even kill Timmy.

MILES RAN INTO THE HOUSE, his nerves on edge. No telling what was happening to Timmy. What if Ables was lurking nearby waiting on him to leave Jordan alone?

He jogged to the office, snatched the fax printouts, then quickly stopped by his cabin for a change of clothes, his passport and his laptop.

Five minutes later when he entered Jordan's cabin, the shower was running. For a moment, he allowed himself to imagine her beneath the spray of water, rivulets trickling over her bare, delicate skin.

A groan of desire mingled with denial. He could not have her.

And even if he could, this was not the time.

His son had been kidnapped. Every second counted.

Banishing the erotic images along with the voice nagging at him that he might be too late for Timmy as he had been for Marie, he spread the printouts on her kitchen table and skimmed the names. First, the list of people in the courtroom during the trial.

Because the press had raised the Slasher to celebrity serial killer status, death threats had come in against Dugan, along with protestors saying the cops had railroaded him just to cover their butts for letting four women's murders go unsolved for so long. The judge had instilled strict security measures. Everyone in the courtroom had been searched and had to provide ID.

Cameras, including cell phones, had been banned.

As soon as he skimmed the names from the trial, he compared them to the visitor's log at the prison. He flipped through the first week's, then the second and found nothing. But on the first day of the third week, a name registered.

Janet Bridges.

She had attended the trial the first two weeks. She had also visited him in jail at the beginning of week three when the defense began to present their side, which had only lasted four days.

But she hadn't been present for the reading of the verdict.

Adrenaline pumped hope through him. He logged on to the police database and plugged in her name. No arrest record.

A little more digging and he discovered she was a real estate broker who had worked with Dugan to expand his businesses. She had a home in Santa Fe.

He dialed her phone number but there was no answer. Next he tried the office number listed, but received a message that she was unavailable.

"Miss Bridges," he said as he drummed his fingers on the counter. "This is Detective Miles McGregor. It's urgent that I speak with you. Please call me back." He left his phone number, then hung up with a frown.

Dugan had mentioned that she didn't believe him. Had she known something about the case that would have helped nail Dugan? Or had she disappeared to cover for him? Could she have killed June Kelly to free Dugan? Would she talk to him when he found her?

Hell yes, she would. He'd make her.

His son's life depended on it.

And if she had helped Dugan with the murders or was hiding him now, he'd make sure she went to jail with him.

JORDAN DRIED OFF, applied antibiotic ointment and a bandage to her shoulder wound, then cleaned the cut on her forehead. Barring makeup, she couldn't do anything to camouflage the bruise on her cheek; it was already turning a nasty purple and black.

But she'd never been vain or taken much time with her appearance, and now wasn't the time to start worrying about it.

She yanked her hair back into a ponytail, dressed in clean jeans and a white shirt and hurried back to the den. Miles was seated at the computer, scribbling on a pad.

"Did you find something?" Jordan asked.

He glanced up, winced as his gaze fell on the bruise on her face, then shrugged. "I think so." He stood. "I think this woman Janet Bridges may have been the woman Dugan talked about. I have an address I'm going to check out."

"Let's go."

"Jordan, no." He moved to her and touched her cheek. "You've been through enough."

"We've already discussed this," Jordan said as she reached for her denim jacket. "I was getting to Dugan. I may be able to help." She squeezed his hand. "Besides, I'm a counselor. If this woman is confused or torn over what to do, she might listen to me before she does the man who put Dugan in jail."

He looked as if he was going to argue, then seemed to accept that she might be right.

"All right, come on."

Jordan nodded, grabbed her purse and followed him to the Jeep. She was tired though and lay her head back and fell asleep on the drive to Santa Fe. When she awakened, Miles was pulling into a row of pricey-looking upscale condos on the outskirts of town.

Janet Bridges must have done well in her job. Either that or Dugan had paid her off.

Miles led Jordan down a brick walkway through an outdoor garden, then up to the front door. He buzzed the doorbell, and they waited, each of them scanning the exterior in search of the woman.

"She might be at her office," Jordan suggested.

"I called but no answer. I left a message. Let's canvass the neighbors. Maybe one of them knows where she is."

They knocked on three doors. An elderly woman with hearing loss answered at the first one, and claimed not to know Janet at all. The other two were empty, the residents probably already at work.

Jordan noticed a young woman in a sports bra and workout pants exiting the condo to the left of Janet's and rushed toward her.

"Excuse me, miss, but can you tell us where Janet Bridges is? We need to talk to her."

A weary look shadowed her eyes. "Who wants to know?"

Miles cleared his throat and flashed his badge. "Ma'am, we have reason to believe she was friends with a man named Robert Dugan."

The young lady visibly took a step back. "I know who he is. Why, has he hurt Janet?"

Jordan read the fear in her tone. Not fear of them but of Dugan. "We don't know yet," Jordan assured her. "But Mr. Dugan kidnapped Detective McGregor's son and we need to find him. We were hoping Miss Bridges might be able to help."

The woman shook her head, eyes flaring with a seed of panic. "Not Janet. Hell, she was terrified of the man. She told him to leave her alone. And when he was released from prison, she moved away so he wouldn't be able to find her."

Jordan grimaced. She hoped this wasn't a dead end. "Do you have any idea where she moved?"

The woman fidgeted, obviously debating whether or not to reveal what she knew.

"Listen, miss," Miles cut in. "Dugan shot and killed a deputy last night and injured another man before he abducted my little boy. He's armed and dangerous and he may be coming after your friend."

The young woman paled. "You don't understand. Janet did love him at first, but when all that stuff came out at the trial…she was freaked out. She's completely terrified of him."

Jordan rubbed her arm. "Please tell us what you know. We promise you we'll protect Miss Bridges."

The girl chewed her thumbnail for a minute, then finally relented. "She made friends with this guy at the gym. His name is Matt Connor."

"Where does he live?"

She took the pad Miles offered and scribbled down the address.

They thanked her then rushed back to the car. Maybe this

Connor guy could point them to Janet and she could lead them to Dugan.

Then they could find Timmy and hopefully bring him back alive.

THE DRIVE TO CONNOR'S place took less than fifteen minutes. But for Miles, it was fifteen minutes of hell.

He swerved into the small neighborhood, silently noting that Connor must not make the kind of money Janet Bridges had. Small ranch houses were nestled on land that had once been farmland, leaving it flat and almost desolate. The summers must be unbearably hot with no trees for shade.

He parked and went around the Jeep to join Jordan. It was almost noon now and the sun had fought through the fog and hazy morning sky, slanting shadows on the sidewalk. The neighborhood seemed quiet: a few cars scattered here and there indicated stay-at-home moms or quite possibly with the economy, the unemployed.

Jordan remained quiet but kept pace with him as they climbed the front stoop. Toys littered the neighbor's yard but Connor's didn't have any, suggesting the man was single and childless.

Maybe he lived alone? Or did Janet Bridges live with him?

Miles raised his fist and knocked, and Jordan tapped her foot while they waited. Miles inched sideways to check the garage and noted an older-model Volvo parked inside.

Hmm, was the man home? Or did he own a second car?

Jordan rang the bell again while he slipped to the side and peeked in the windows. Furniture in place, but no sign of anyone there.

Curious, he motioned to Jordan to follow him, and they walked around back. No fence, no guard dog... The back door was open.

Instincts born from years of police work kicked in, and

he motioned for Jordan to stay back. She nodded, obviously sensing something was wrong.

Gun at the ready, he stepped into the threshold of the doorway. The moment he did, the stench of death hit him.

A second cautious step inside, and he saw blood splattered across the floor. He felt Jordan behind him as he slowly moved forward. Then he spotted a man's body on the floor.

Dammit. It had to be Connor.

He'd been shot in the head, his brain matter and blood covering the floor and dotting the walls in a sickening spray.

Chapter Seventeen

Jordan gasped at the sight of the dead man.

Miles threw up his arm to keep her behind him. "Step back outside, and don't touch anything, Jordan. I need to see if the woman's here."

Jordan nodded, her heart pounding as she backed out on the stoop to wait. She understood his concern—this was a crime scene now. They couldn't contaminate the evidence or it might interfere with arresting and prosecuting the killer.

What about Janet Bridges? Was she dead in there as well?

Had Dugan killed them both?

She jammed her hands in the pockets of her jacket to keep from clutching the railing and scanned the backyard in case the killer was watching. Two houses over, she spotted a woman pushing a small child in a swing. A dog barked in the distance, starting a chorus as other neighborhood dogs joined in.

Trees shook in the breeze, then a shadow moved.

She froze, prepared to scream for Miles, but the man moved into view and she realized it was the mailman.

She exhaled a sigh of relief, then paced the yard, her senses alert for strangers. Five minutes passed, then ten, then fifteen. Where was Miles?

What if the killer had been waiting and ambushed him? She hadn't heard a gunshot or any commotion...

She stepped back up to the doorway and called his name. "Miles, are you okay?"

Footsteps pounded on the wood floor, then he appeared, frowning.

Jordan wanted to rush to him and throw her arms around him, to feel him next to her, living and breathing. "I was worried."

"Sorry." He shrugged. "The woman's not here, but I did a quick search to see if there was any clue as to where she is or where Dugan might go."

"Did you find anything?"

He shook his head. "No. I even checked the man's message machine but there was nothing."

"How about a cell phone or computer?" Jordan asked.

"No cell. If he had one, the killer must have taken it. I looked at his computer but didn't find any references to Janet Bridges."

"If she was hiding from Dugan, maybe she changed her name or they used a code."

Miles worked his mouth side to side. "Probably. I have to call this in and get a forensics team to process the scene." He called the number, identified himself, then explained about the body and gave the police the address.

"Yes, he was dead when I arrived. No sign of the killer or the woman Janet Bridges." He explained his reasons for being there as he carefully sidestepped the body.

Minutes later, a siren wailed and a police car careened down the street and into the drive. Miles peeled off his gloves and jammed them in the inside pocket of his jacket, then took Jordan's arm and escorted her around front to meet the police.

He stowed his weapon and identified himself as soon as the uniformed officer exited his patrol car.

"Detective McGregor. I called in the murder." He flashed

his badge and the two officers approached. "This is Jordan Keys."

"Officers Rameriz and Stoner," the heavier cop said by way of introduction. "What were you two doing here?"

"The man who lived here was friends with a female who was once close to Robert Dugan. We thought she might know where he was headed."

Another car drove up, and a man wearing a gray suit and wire-rimmed glasses strode toward them carrying a medical bag. "Assistant medical examiner Carson Pullman," the man said. "Where's the body?"

Miles gestured toward the house. "Kitchen. In the back."

Officer Stoner followed the medical examiner while Officer Rameriz took their statement. "Did you touch anything inside?"

Miles shook his head. "I did a sweep through in search of the woman and to make sure the house was clear, then put on gloves and checked the computer."

Rameriz raised a brow. "How did you get in?"

"We knocked on the front door but there was no answer, so we walked around back. The door was open."

"Unlocked?" Rameriz asked. This time he angled his head toward Jordan for confirmation.

"Yes," she said. "And before you ask, no, I didn't go inside. When Miles spotted the blood, he told me to stay outside while he made sure the killer was gone."

Rameriz gave a short nod and closed his notepad. "All right. Thanks for calling it in."

"You'll get a forensics team to process the scene, won't you?" Miles asked.

Rameriz nodded. "They should be here any minute."

"I did a preliminary check of the man's computer, but didn't find anything. Ask them to look for any references to a woman named Janet Bridges. Also any family member's name, or mention of Robert Dugan."

"You think she was helping Dugan?" Rameriz asked.

Miles made a hissing sound. "I don't know. Her girlfriend claims she was running from him. My guess is, he tracked her here and killed this guy to try to find her." He tipped his Stetson as if to shade his eyes. "Whether or not Connor gave her up before Dugan offed him is the question. And if we find her, she might have information to help us nail Dugan on the other murders."

"You're sure he did this?" Rameriz asked. "Maybe Janet Bridges killed Connor and she's joined Dugan."

Jordan considered that possibility. "At this point we can't be sure," she admitted. "For all we know, he killed the boyfriend, then forced her to go with him."

Rameriz chewed over her suggestion. "I'll have the team search the computer, his car, his phone records and see what we can find."

Miles's phone buzzed at his waist. He thanked the officer, then checked the caller ID box. "I need to get this."

He turned away for a second, spoke into the phone, then clicked it off and turned back, his body jumpy. "Dugan has been spotted near the border. We have to go."

He grabbed Jordan's hand and they rushed to his Jeep.

MILES'S MIND RACED with panic as he drove down the highway. If Dugan had been here and killed Connor, had he found Janet Bridges? Had he killed her or kidnapped her? If so, maybe she would at least keep Timmy safe....

"Where were they spotted?" Jordan asked.

"Near Rio Grande City."

Jordan checked her watch. "He's making good time."

"Yeah, especially to have stopped here looking for his old girlfriend." He tossed his Stetson to the seat and scrubbed his hand through his hair. "Why would he take the time to do that? He knows we're after him. He has a hostage. And he must know she's been hiding from him. It doesn't make sense."

"I don't know," Jordan said, although her brows were pinched in thought. "He and I discussed his mother and the fact that he didn't have a father. I think the lack of that family is deeply rooted in his psychosis."

Miles cursed. He didn't want to understand Dugan, and he especially didn't want to hear some sob story about how bad he had it growing up.

Dammit, he'd had a rough life, too, and so had half the men he knew. Especially the ones who'd started the BBL.

But that hadn't turned them into serial killers.

"I don't see how this helps," he admitted in frustration.

Jordan pressed a hand to his arm. "Understanding his behavior, his reasons for his sickness, can be useful when we catch him. We can use those details to help calm him and get him to turn himself in."

"You're talking about profiling, aren't you?"

Jordan nodded. "It works."

"So how does it explain what he's done now? The fact that he took time out to hunt for Bridges gave us more time to track him."

"His actions may not make sense to us, but in his mind, they're logical. But if we follow his thought process we can predict his next movements." Jordan tapped her fingernails on her thigh. "What if he always wanted that happy family, a mother to love him, a child of his own?"

"I'm not following." He sure as hell didn't want the bastard raising Timmy.

"Maybe I started him thinking about his mother. The reason he wants her dead is so he can kill the source of his pain."

"That makes sense." In a demented way.

"He said you ruined his life, his future. What if he's planning his future after he murders his mother?" She twisted her hands together. "He loved this woman Janet so once the slate is cleared by getting rid of his mother, he wants to build a life with her. Maybe have that happy family."

Miles saw red. "Him and Bridges and Timmy. That's what you're suggesting."

Jordan sighed and tucked a strand of her hair behind her ear. "If that's his mindset, Miles, it means he won't hurt Timmy."

His chest ached, but he latched onto the hope she offered, no matter how irrational it sounded to him. He had to.

Thinking that Timmy might be dead was something he couldn't live with.

He would keep looking for him. And he would find him.

And bring him home.

Jordan squeezed his hand, and he squeezed hers in turn, grateful she was with him. If she wasn't, he'd be falling apart.

"Miles, there was something else about Dugan that struck me as odd. He had a nervous tic, and his eyes…seemed funny, glazed, almost glassy as if he was on medication."

"He's a psycho," Miles said flatly.

"Yes, but at the trial he didn't exhibit any of those signs. It makes me wonder if he's sick. An illness might explain some of his behavior. It could have incited him to come after you instead of resuming his life once he was freed."

"I don't give a damn about his health," Miles snapped.

"Just consider the possibility," Jordan said. "Call your friend and have him find out if Dugan had had any recent medical issues. An illness might have pushed him over the edge into coming after you."

"He came after me for revenge," Miles said.

"Just check," Jordan said. "It might be important later."

Miles cursed but called Blackpaw, explained Jordan's theory and asked him to look into Dugan's medical records. Mason agreed.

"Have you found Ables?" Miles asked.

"I'm five minutes from his last known address," Blackpaw said. "And I did find out that Dugan's real mother was still alive. Her name was CeeCee."

"Thanks."

Miles disconnected and rubbed a hand through his hair. They rode the next hour in silence, the air thick with worry and fear. All Miles could think about was that Dugan had increased the distance between them.

That even though Jordan thought he might be planning this fictional deluded life with the Bridges woman and his son, Dugan was essentially crazy.

Crazy, volatile, desperate. Not a good combination.

Desperate people did desperate things when cornered.

Dugan was like a time bomb waiting to explode. All it would take was the wrong person, the wrong comment, someone trying to stop him, to push his trigger, and he might ignite and hurt Timmy.

Early-evening shadows hovered above the city as they approached, the open space and wilderness giving way to gas stations, motels and small housing developments.

Rio Grande City had once epitomized the Wild West. But civilization and progress had made its mark. Miles frowned. Not always a good thing.

Worse, Rio Grande City was too close to the border for comfort.

Jordan rubbed her shoulder, and a seed of guilt nagged at Miles. "Are you sure you're okay?"

"Just tired," Jordan said. "I'll grab some water and take a painkiller when we stop." She seemed to be studying the passing scenery as if she might spot Dugan and Timmy somewhere in the mesquites dotting the side of the road. "Where was he last seen?"

"There." Miles pointed to the convenience store ahead,

then swerved into the parking lot. Jordan and he climbed out and walked up to the store entrance.

A bell tinkled as they entered, and on instinct, Miles scanned the store for trouble. A couple of teenagers hovering by the magazine rack, probably looking for *Playboy*. A trucker buying cigarettes. Two women in too-tight jeans and shirts tied at their waists, who looked as if they'd been rode hard and put up wet, leaving the bathroom.

Miles strode up to the Native American woman behind the counter. Her gray hair dangled in a braid down her back, her dress hung on skin that was leathery and sagging. Half of her teeth had rotted out. She could have been sixty or ninety—he couldn't tell. But life had definitely been rough on her.

He removed his badge from his pocket and introduced himself, then handed her a flyer Blackpaw had faxed with the other papers showing a picture of Robert Dugan. "Ma'am, you were the person who reported that you spotted this man, Robert Dugan?"

Her gnarled fingers curled around the printout as she studied it. It was Dugan's mug shot alongside a photo of him at the trial. Hell though, for all he knew, Dugan could be wearing a disguise by now.

The trucker lumbered outside to his eighteen-wheeler and the two women followed, while Jordan combed the aisles for water and aspirin.

"Yeah, that was him."

Panic warred with relief inside Miles. "He had a little boy with him?" He showed her Timmy's picture next. Just the sight of it nearly brought him to his knees.

She chewed on her lower lip for a minute, then wrinkled her nose. "Can't say I saw the boy."

Jordan moved up beside him and slid her hand to his arm for support.

"You didn't see the little boy at all?" Miles asked in a choked voice.

She shook her head. "No, sir. Like I told that other cop come by, man in the picture left the police car outside and stole a pickup in the parking lot."

"A pickup?"

"Yeah, belonged to my boy. He lets me drive it to work. Gonna be real mad it got took."

Jordan rubbed his back. "Are you sure you didn't see the little boy? Maybe he stayed low, or maybe the man had him wrapped in a blanket?"

"I'm sorry." The woman scratched her brow. "But that truck…Billy had a storage bin in the cab. Covered with a tarp."

"So he could have put Timmy in it and driven off?" Jordan asked.

The woman nodded. "I reckon he could have. But I didn't hear nothing. No kid screaming or crying, I mean."

Miles gripped the counter. If Timmy had been wrapped up and hadn't been fighting or making noise, he might be hurt.

Or worse…

No, he couldn't think like that.

But even as he ordered himself to be positive, seeds of doubt sprouted in his mind. If Timmy hadn't been with him, what had Dugan done with him?

Had he killed him and left him somewhere along the way? Somewhere out in the miles and miles of wilderness where they might not find him for days?

Chapter Eighteen

Jordan felt the sense of despair pummeling Miles, and knew she had to do something.

She had been too late for her brother, but she would not be too late for Miles's son. Or him.

She slid her hands up, cupped his face and forced him to look at her. "Listen to me, Miles. The fact that this woman didn't see Timmy doesn't mean he's not alive." She made her voice strong. "Do you hear me? Timmy is still out there and we will find him. I do not believe that Dugan hurt him. I just don't."

Miles heaved a sigh and searched her face, his expression so tormented that she dragged him into a hug. "Listen to me. We can't give up. Timmy needs us to be strong and smart about this."

"You're right." A shudder coursed through him, shaking her to the core with its intensity. He took a deep breath, stiffened and turned back to the woman. "I understand you didn't see the boy, ma'am, but did you see which direction Dugan drove?"

Her wrinkles deepened as she angled her head to the left. "He went south."

Toward the border, exactly where Jordan and Miles knew he would go.

"Thank you," Jordan said as she took Miles's arm and

pulled him outside. "Come on, we need to go. You can alert the authorities that Dugan is coming, and maybe they'll arrest him at the border."

Miles jerked himself from his fear-induced stupor and nodded, then reached for his phone as they rushed back to his Jeep. He called his lieutenant as he started the engine, then explained where they were.

Jordan fastened her seat belt, well aware of Miles's terseness as he argued with his superior over what he should do.

"Of course this is personal," Miles said. "But I'm not turning back. You can have my badge, but I'm going to find Dugan and bring my boy home."

Jordan looked out the window at the darkening sky and prayed they would find Timmy.

That she hadn't been wrong about Dugan—that they'd bring Timmy home alive.

MILES LATCHED ONTO THE HOPE Jordan's words had offered like a lifeline. She was right. He couldn't give up.

He couldn't lose his boy.

Night had set in, the city lights glittering, the evening crowd of tourists and locals making the traffic thick. He cut through the side streets, weaving around slower cars, and blowing past a stalled vehicle.

He would get Timmy back and take him fishing, and buy him that horse that he'd promised him. And they'd get a dog and a ranch and spend hours together working the horses and just…hanging out by the creek.

Yes, he had to have a creek on the property and stables and when Timmy was older they might spring for a four-wheeler.

Sucking in a calming breath, he focused on the road. A minute later, his cell phone rang. He yanked it open, hoping the caller had answers that would lead to his son.

"Miles, it's Blackpaw. Our computer guys called. You were right. Dugan had some tests run when he got out of prison."

Miles ground his jaw. He didn't give a damn. Except for how it might help him find the bastard. "And?"

"He has a brain tumor. Inoperable."

"So he's tying up unfinished business before he croaks." He saw Jordan frown. "Anything else?"

"Yeah. Ables wasn't at his house. Looks like he packed a suitcase, and judging from his computer, he booked a flight to Mexico himself. Airport authorities are waiting to pick him up."

Stupid son of a bitch probably thought the cops hadn't made the connection yet. At least Miles hoped that was what he thought.

Then they could catch him and find out exactly how many women he had killed.

And why he'd helped his half brother when nothing in their investigative research had shown that the two of them were close.

Miles's phone buzzed again. "Let me know when you arrest him," he said. "I have another call coming in."

He clicked over to answer the other call. "McGregor."

"It's Special Agent Graham Storm," the man said. "I'm a friend of Mason Blackpaw's."

Miles tensed. "Yeah?"

"Robert Dugan just blew through the border. He's in Mexico."

Miles pounded his fist on the steering wheel, nearly losing control of the vehicle. Jordan gripped the wheel to right the vehicle and gave him a panicked, questioning look.

"Dammit," Miles said, gathering his composure. "I think his mother lives there. Her first name is CeeCee. Can you find an address?"

"I'll get back to you ASAP."

Sweat beaded on his brow as he ended the call and sped up.

"What was that about?" Jordan asked.

"You were right." Miles took the road leading out of town, speeding up to pass a truck that was about to pull out in front of him. "Dugan has a brain tumor."

Jordan fidgeted with a lock of her hair. "That might explain the tic, and why he's been behaving so erratically."

"As opposed to his methodical, sadistic kills."

Jordan nodded, her expression troubled. "It also explains why he's going to see his mother now. Time is running out for him."

And maybe for Timmy.

But Miles bit back the words. He couldn't allow himself to believe that.

Jordan didn't comment further either. She turned and studied the passing scenery while he focused on the road. The miles crawled by, but finally he neared the border. The border patrol was on full alert, official *policía* vehicles in abundance, traffic clogged as the patrolmen checked passports and inspected vehicles.

Agent Storm was supposed to alert the authorities he was on his way, so he pulled to the side, stepped from the car and approached one of the officers.

The officer immediately looked wary, his hand poised on his weapon. Miles had already removed his ID and passport and held both of them for identification purposes. "Miles Mc-Gregor. Special Agent Graham Storm of the FBI was supposed to contact you about me. I'm here to meet with your authorities about a man named Robert Dugan. He's wanted for kidnapping a child. I've just been alerted that he crossed the border."

The officer examined his ID, ordered him to stay put, went to speak with another officer, then returned. "One of our *policía* officers is waiting to meet with you across the border.

Pull your car up here and we'll check your passports, then you can be on your way."

"Thank you." Miles quickly returned to his Jeep, drove to the checkpoint, then handed him their passports. The officer scrutinized their paperwork and his badge, then finally let them pass.

Another *policía* officer pulled up in front of him and escorted him to the nearest police station. They passed several trucks and cars and a tourist bus as they entered the small town, then wove through the village where locals sold their wares. Other small stores, a cantina, gift shop, cigar shop and beer store occupied one row while the police station sat at the far end of the town.

The small adobe structure looked worn and was overgrown with weeds. Frustration knotted his insides.

Hell, he didn't want to deal with the police here. If he found Dugan he wanted to kill him without worrying about the rules.

The Mexican police were known for taking bribes to supplement their poor pay, too, but since his business with them wasn't related to drugs, he hoped for assistance.

The officer who'd led them to the station climbed out and escorted them up the dimly lit path to the doorway. Dirt and weathered patches made the building look ancient, and as Miles entered, he scanned the front room that consisted of dingy concrete walls and floors.

The place reeked of sweat, cigarettes and filth. A short robust Hispanic man in uniform with a bulbous nose and thick mustache stood, tugging at his too-tight uniform. "Officer Sanchez," the man said in greeting.

Miles introduced the two of them. "You know why we're here?"

"Sí." Sanchez gestured toward his desk where a faxed photo of Dugan and Timmy lay. "Your FBI call, he say this man wanted for kidnapping your son."

"That's right," Miles said, antsy to skip the chitchat and find Dugan. "We have reason to believe that his mother lives here, and that he's on his way to visit her. I hope you can help us track her down."

"*Sí,* we will try." The man rubbed at his thick mustache, then gestured toward the ancient computer on his desk. "Unfortunately we do not have the fancy equipment you do, but our federal police division has better. I contact them and let you know."

Miles clenched his teeth in frustration. That could take days. Days he might not have.

"Where will you be staying?" Sanchez asked.

Miles glanced at Jordan with a frown. "I'm not sure. But you can reach me on my cell phone." He scribbled down the number and handed it to the officer. "Please check your records for information on Dugan's mother. Her name is CeeCee Dugan. I think she's a prostitute."

The man's eyebrows rose, making his mustache twitch. "If she is as you say, she may not have a steady address. But there is a whorehouse where many of the locals work."

Miles's pulse picked up. "Where is that?"

Sanchez rolled a cigar between his fingers. "I tell you, but you don't give girls no trouble. They see you and think arrest and run."

"I'm here to get my son back, not arrest your street girls," Miles said. He'd use whomever he had to in order to find Timmy.

Sanchez studied him for a moment, but finally conceded. "The cantina is the pickup spot. The Red Hot motel at the end of the street is where the girls take the johns. That is, unless they do them in the back room."

Miles thanked him again, then took Jordan's arm and led her outside.

Jordan pulled her jacket around her. "Even if she once worked that street, she might not be working there now."

Of course he knew that.

"Dugan is thirty-five so she might be in her fifties or older by now," Jordan continued. "If age hasn't deteriorated her appeal as a hooker, she might have succumbed to some disease she picked up from one of her johns."

"True," Miles said. "But if she's near this town or worked here before, one of the other girls might know where she is now."

At least he hoped that was the case. They needed a damn break.

Night had set in and Timmy had to be terrified.

He didn't want him to have to spend the night with a monster.

JORDAN COULD FEEL Miles's tension because her own body was riddled with anxiety, too. Night loomed long and lonely, the darkness a reminder that Timmy was out in the unknown with Dugan and not with his father where he belonged.

The wilderness between them and the next town meant they could be anywhere by now.

Every hour, day and mile that passed would make it more difficult to find Timmy.

And lessened their chances of finding him alive.

What if Dugan's tumor affected him to the point that he lost all senses and killed Timmy?

Shivering with worry, she followed Miles to the Jeep and climbed in, hoping they weren't chasing a dead lead. But they had nothing else to go on.

"You can wait in the car if you want while I go in," Miles said.

Jordan shook her head. "No, I might be able to help."

Miles looked doubtful, but he was running on emotions and didn't argue.

He drove to the cantina and parked. They went to the door together. "Be careful, Jordan. Watch your drink and stay close to me."

Jordan wanted to tell him she wasn't a fool, but she refrained. He didn't need her testiness now. He needed some clue as to how to find his son.

The place was dimly lit, authentic Mexican decor with sombreros, maracas and cacti decorating the orange-and-yellow adobe walls. The bar held dozens of patrons, mostly men, while the restaurant section catered more to couples, although the place's reputation must be known in the area because there were few families.

Two men at the end of the bar gave her lewd looks while a scantily clad woman in red eyed her from the back area, where a string of Mexican beads dangled over a doorway to the back room.

Another female in thigh-high boots, a low-cut spandex top and miniskirt poured tequila through a funnel into a man's throat in a corner.

Miles slid onto a barstool and motioned to the bartender for two beers. Jordan excused herself to go to the ladies' room while he spoke with the bartender and a local man sitting beside him.

She spied the woman in red watching Miles. Sensing trouble, she veered by the ladies' room and decided to confront her.

"Miss?"

The woman started to duck behind the beads, but Jordan caught her arm. "Please, wait. I need to speak with you."

At close range, she realized the woman was much younger than she originally thought, probably early twenties. Already she looked aged from the hardships of her lifestyle. "What do you want?" the woman asked, trying for bravado. "You and your *policía* friend come here to shut us down, take our jobs."

"No, that's not why we're here." How had she known Miles was police? "Did someone warn you we were coming?"

The girl shrugged. "I recognize a pig when I see one."

Jordan softened her grip. "You have it all wrong. That man is a detective but not here in Mexico. And he didn't come to arrest you or expose this place."

The wariness in the girl's eyes dissipated slightly, and Jordan released her hold. "Then why you come?"

"Because of a man named Robert Dugan, a man who has murdered many people and kidnapped Mr. McGregor's son. Timmy's only five." Jordan paused, pleading with her eyes. "He's in terrible danger and we're trying to find him. We traced him across the border."

The young girl shifted and fidgeted with her hands. "You think he come here?"

Jordan glanced around the place. "I don't know. Maybe, maybe not. His mother lived in Mexico, and we think she might have been a…working girl."

The young woman's eyes widened.

"Her name was CeeCee. Her son is thirty-five so she would be older than you."

"CeeCee," the young woman said. "No one name her here."

Jordan gave her arm a squeeze. "Thank you anyway. If you hear anything about this man—" she removed the printout of Dugan's face and showed it to her "—please let us know." She jotted Miles's cell phone number and name on the handout and gave it to the woman, then ducked into the bathroom.

By the time she finished washing her hands, the woman suddenly appeared in the bathroom. "I show to others," she said quietly. "One of the girls say she go by Candy. She was here but gone year ago."

Jordan's pulse pounded. "Do you know where she went?"

The girl shoved a small piece of paper in her hand, an
Jordan realized it was an address. "Left with man who cam
through. Live with him."

Jordan thanked her and rushed to tell Miles. He looke
grim, but asked the bartender the man's name.

"Cortez, he mean," the bartender said. "But he like Cand
and say he keep her for himself."

"I have his address." Jordan pushed it into Miles's han
and he motioned toward the door.

"Let's go."

Jordan's stomach churned as she slid into the Jeep, an
they drove away from the small town. Soon the buildings gav
way to desolate land and patches of poverty-ridden areas tha
made Jordan sad for the people who lived in the tiny rottin
dwellings. They passed a section of concrete houses that ha
fallen into disrepair and were abandoned, then Miles turne
onto a road that seemed to lead nowhere.

A chill enveloped her as the endless emptiness, darknes
and barren land swallowed them. "Are you sure we're goin
the right way?"

"According to the GPS, yes." Miles rubbed at his nec
where she was sure the tension was knotting his muscles. He
own was cramped and aching from fatigue.

They lapsed into silence, the narrow road winding deepe
into the wilderness, but finally Jordan spotted a set of build
ings that looked like a compound ahead.

"There," she said. "That has to be it."

Miles sped up, both of them surveying the buildings, whic
at first sight appeared dark and empty.

Despair threatened as she twisted in her seat.

"I don't see any cars or lights."

"Dugan could have hidden the car inside the compound

"You think he knows we've followed him here?"

Miles shrugged. "I think he's delusional and paranoid an

knows he's a wanted man. He'll do whatever he can to hide himself."

Jordan clung to hope as he slowed the Jeep and pulled up to the compound. The metal gate was open, and as he slowed, she saw no cars inside the premises. No sign of movement or life.

Night shadows hugged the tattered walls, but the headlights from Miles's Jeep fell on peeling paint, overgrown weeds and a sign saying Casa Laredo that hung askew, blowing in the wind, all confirming that no one lived here year-round.

Apprehension knotted her insides as Miles cut the lights and pulled to a stop. He grabbed a flashlight and his gun, then opened the car door and stepped outside.

MILES INCHED FORWARD, his senses alert. "Jordan, wait in the car."

She glanced around at the desolate area with a grimace. "No way. I'll feel safer with you."

He sighed. "All right, but stay behind me."

"Yes, sir."

He cut her a sharp look at her sarcastic tone, then realized she was simply tired and worried the same as him. Worse, she had been physically assaulted, a bullet had skimmed her arm, and yet, she'd rallied, fought for his son and been a rock for him.

She was the most courageous woman he'd ever met.

He didn't know how to thank her.

But he didn't have time to think about it now. He scanned the flashlight along the ground and spotted fresh footprints in the dirt.

His heart hammered. "Someone was here."

"You're right." Rocks skittered below Jordan's boots as she followed him. "There's more over there."

She pointed to the side entrance, and he followed the trail. A man's prints. No child's.

A hollow emptiness tore at him. Dugan could have been carrying Timmy.

No. He refused to let the images and possibilities in his mind.

Instead, he turned the knob on the ramshackle wooden door and it squeaked open. Sweat beaded on his neck and trickled downward as he shined the flashlight inside and followed the dirt tracks. The concrete floor was worn and showed signs that an animal had been inside through a mudroom, then a small hallway leading to a den and kitchen combination. The furniture left behind had been chewed and picked by birds and God knew what else.

He held his gun at the ready in case Dugan was still here waiting to ambush him. The sound of the wind whipping through the stone walls echoed around him.

Then he spotted a T-shirt on the floor of the den. A green T-shirt that looked like the one Timmy had been wearing when Dugan had snatched him.

His breath stalled in his chest as he knelt to examine it.

Dammit.

No…

Blood dotted the shirt and a note had been pinned to the sleeve.

Say goodbye to your son, McGregor. I won.

Chapter Nineteen

Miles doubled over as pain and denial ripped through him. No...Timmy could not be dead.

He couldn't be.

A loud groan punctuated the air, and somewhere on a distant level he realized it had come from him. His chest heaved for air, the room swirled with an icy darkness that beckoned and bile rose to his throat.

He thought he was going to vomit and pushed to his feet, staggered outside and hung his head over the side of the concrete walkway. Dragging in a huge gulp of air, he fought the nausea.

Then he felt Jordan's hand on his back. Her fingers slowly rubbing the base of his neck.

"Miles, Timmy...he may still be out there. Dugan could just be toying with you."

He spun toward her, his heart beating frantically, panic paralyzing him. Tears must have leaked from his eyes because she lifted one hand and wiped at his cheeks.

For a moment he was so dizzy he couldn't see.

She gripped his jaw with her hands and kissed him gently. "Listen to what I said. Dugan is sick. He may just be tormenting you. Otherwise, where's Timmy's body?"

Her words made him buckle over again, and she caught

him and wrapped her arms around him. Pain wrenched him
so deeply it cut at his soul.

"I know you're scared," Jordan said firmly. "But pull it
together, Miles. We need to search the house. He could have
tied Timmy up somewhere and left him here." She jerked his
face up. "Don't give up, do you hear me? Let's look around
in case he's here. If he is, he needs us to find him."

Her stern voice shattered the panicked terror overwhelming him, and he nodded. Dragging in a breath, he jumped into
motion and began to search the compound.

They used his flashlight and crept through the big block
house, combing room to room, checking closets and storage
units and even searching for a trap or secret door. But an hour
later Miles knew the place was empty.

There were two smaller buildings, one a garage where some
old tools had been stored, the second a space that looked as
if it had been used as a drug lab. The scent of chemicals still
lingered behind.

Finally Miles gave in to defeat. "He's not here." He scanned
the property. "Unless he's out there somewhere."

Jordan shuddered, but shook her head. "We won't stop
looking, Miles. Call the local police and ask them to organize
a search team. We can't possibly search the area by ourselves."

Miles agreed, phoned Sanchez and filled him in.

"It will be impossible to get a search team there at this
hour," Sanchez said. "But I will have men there at dawn."

Miles wanted to lay into him and order men to come out
now, but it was pitch-dark and they had miles to cover where
Dugan could have left Timmy. If they waited until morning
they could get a chopper and cover more ground.

He just hoped Dugan had lied, and that it wouldn't be too
late.

That he hadn't hurt Timmy or left him out in the elements
alone to die.

His phone buzzed, and he snapped it open.

"Miles, it's Blackpaw."

"Please tell me you have good news," he said gruffly.

A long sigh echoed back. "I'm afraid not."

Miles braced himself. "Then what?"

"It's about Belsa."

"You found him?"

"Not exactly. But one of Marie's neighbors saw Ables's photo on the news, and guess what?"

He cursed. He was in no mood for games. "Just tell me, dammit."

"Belsa and Ables are the same man."

Miles gritted his teeth. God…Marie had had no idea she'd been dating Dugan's half brother. That he'd probably stalked her, even introduced himself to her and his son, so he could be close to them to help his brother.

So had he killed Marie or had Dugan?

JORDAN'S HEART POUNDED as Miles relayed the news about Belsa.

He was so upset, Jordan took his arm and pulled him toward the Jeep. "Get in, I'll drive."

Miles shook his head in protest, but she shoved him into the passenger side and he was so weary and in such a fog that he let her.

She checked the GPS and found a motel the next city over and headed to it.

Jordan wanted to alleviate Miles's pain, but the truth was she had experienced the same blinding, terrible grief after losing her little brother, and that type of shock robbed you of your breath and senses.

But Timmy wasn't dead. She wouldn't believe it until they found his body.

Her counseling instincts warned her not to give Miles false

hope, but she refused to listen to them. If he gave up and Timmy was out there, Timmy needed them to keep looking.

Miles sat in a stony silence as she drove, the silence deafening as the tires churned over desolate stretches of pocked road. Finally a sweep of buildings cropped into view, the lights of another small town dotting the distance.

Jordan headed into town, found the motel and tried to ignore the rugged, dirty accommodations as she and Miles checked in.

The man behind the desk gave her a lecherous smile when he realized they had no luggage, but she ignored him and asked for one room anyway. Let him think what he would. She didn't give a damn.

All she cared about now was finding Timmy and comforting Miles.

He rallied enough to look around warily as they made their way to the room, his hand close to his gun at all times. Jordan opened the door and winced at the bare furnishings, then shrugged it off.

"Are you hungry?" she asked. "I can go down and pick us up some food."

"I can't eat anything." Miles clenched her hand. "And you aren't going anywhere in this town alone, Jordan. It's not safe."

She gathered that, but she wanted to help.

His body shuddered against her, and she slid a hand up to cup his cheek. "Go shower. We'll rest and start over in the morning. Maybe we'll hear something more by then, get another lead."

Or meet the search team to look for Timmy.

Miles's despondent look indicated that he was thinking the same thing.

"Come on, a shower will do us both good." She took his hand and coaxed him into the tiny bathroom. Under other circumstances, she wouldn't have dared step foot in the shower stall of a roach motel, but tonight the conditions didn't matter.

Miles stood ramrod straight, his body rigid as she reached for his shirt and began to unbutton it. "Jordan—"

"Shh, let me."

His dark gaze latched with hers, emotions brimming to the surface. Pain. Need. Fear.

Hunger.

She couldn't do any more about finding Timmy tonight but she could do this. She raised herself on tiptoe and dragged her mouth to his.

MILES SHUT ALL THE DARK thoughts from his mind. He had to. It was the only way he could keep from throwing himself against a wall.

Or eating his gun.

And neither would help him find his son.

Jordan's words taunted him—Timmy might still be alive. Dugan could be playing them.

The bastard was just cruel enough to pull that kind of sick stunt.

Jordan's other theory nagged at him, too. Dugan might be planning to create his own little family with Timmy....

Over his dead body.

Jordan closed her lips over his, and a surge of white-hot need raged through him. Adrenaline mingled with raw desire, and he tunneled his hands in her hair, ripped out the ponytail holder and spread the luscious strands over her shoulders just as he'd wanted to do since he'd first met her.

He'd tried to deny it but he'd craved her for days now.

Finally she was in his arms. He ached to have her below him, whispering his name while he pounded himself inside her.

Driven by his hunger, he stripped off her shirt while she

tore off his. Their jeans came next, the sound of her zipper sliding down an erotic tease that threatened to make him explode.

Somewhere in the distance, a voice murmured that this was wrong. That he should slow down. Show her some tenderness.

But Jordan's breathy sighs and moans weren't sounds of protest. In fact, she raked her nails over his bare chest as if she wanted him just as he wanted her.

That need fueled his desire even more, and he walked her backward and pressed her against the wall. Boots and socks flew off.

Her underwear came next. Fast and heady, he stripped her, drinking in the sight of her rosy nipples begging for his attention. His sex hardened as she ground herself into him and rubbed his thigh with her bare foot.

He cupped her butt in his hands, caressing her naked flesh and wishing he had the willpower to take it slow and easy, to pleasure her the way she deserved, but a raw ache throbbed through him.

He had to have her now.

She nipped at his neck, and he lowered his head and drew one nipple into his mouth, sucking it until she buckled and cried his name, begging him for more.

He slipped one hand between her legs, parting her thighs for his invasion. Her damp center sent a surge of blood through his groin, and his sex jutted out, thick and needy.

She shoved down his boxers, then wrapped one soft hand around his hard length and pulled him toward her.

He groaned, then lifted her with his hands until she wound her legs around him and he thrust into her.

One squeeze of her legs around him and he felt as if he might come. But he forced his body to still until he regained control.

Jordan had lost control herself though. She dug her fingers

into his shoulders as she impaled herself on his length again, then lifted herself and did it once more. A moan of pleasure ripped from his gut, and the walls shook as she rode him hard, and he drove himself deeper and deeper into her.

He felt the first spasms of her orgasm as her muscles clenched his sex, and he tilted her head back, plunged his tongue into her mouth and tasted her one more time as she came apart in his arms.

The thrill of her cry piercing the air drove him to thrust harder, and he threw her on the bed, pulled her legs wide apart and plunged so deeply he felt her core.

Her body shuddered and shivered around him as he moaned her name and lost himself inside her.

PLEASURE ROLLED THROUGH Jordan in waves. But mingled with the pleasure, intermittent waves of reality rippled through her.

Miles sighed and rolled sideways, pulling her into his embrace, and she allowed herself to nestle in his arms for a few minutes. Emotions she had no business feeling stole through her thoughts.

She was in love with Miles.

She closed her eyes, wondering when it had happened, but she couldn't remember one definable moment. It was all the little ones that had built up. The sexy look in his eyes when he spoke. The possessive, protective aura that radiated from him when it came to his son. The steely strength and determination to protect the world and seek justice for innocents.

He rubbed his forehead against hers and made a low sound in his throat. "I'm sorry, Jordan, I—"

"Shh." She pressed her finger to his lips, then looked up at him and kissed him with all the love that had built in her heart. "We both needed that. No questions. No regrets."

He searched her face for a long moment, then gave a small nod, his eyes blurred with tears that he wouldn't let fall.

She took his hand and kissed his fingers one by one, then placed it over her heart. For a moment they lay entwined, each seeking strength and solace from the other. But his fingers slowly inched over her nipple, teasing it until it stiffened and hunger flared inside his eyes.

Hot need flooded her body with desire, and she kissed him again, then climbed on top of him and drove him to sweet oblivion once again.

An hour later, they collapsed into a deep exhausted sleep. But Jordan jerked awake to the sound of Miles's phone buzzing on the nightstand where he'd dropped it.

Knowing Miles needed rest, she reached for it and pressed the connect button.

"It's Blackpaw. Miles?"

"This is Jordan," she said. "Miles is asleep. Finally." Jordan explained about the night before and the search team they'd ordered.

"Dammit," Blackpaw said. "I hope they don't find anything. But I have some information for him."

"Tell me and I'll let him know."

Blackpaw hesitated, then spoke in a gruff voice. "All right. Maybe it's better he hear it from you. We arrested Ables."

"Dugan's half brother?"

"Yeah, and he confessed to killing June Kelly. He said he grew up in Dugan's shadow and that he wanted to be like him. So he killed Kelly to free his brother. Then he wanted to hook up and work with him but Dugan ignored him and came after Miles."

"Did he kill Timmy's mother?" Jordan asked.

"No, Dugan did."

Just as Miles suspected.

"There's more. Ables gave me an address where he last saw their mother. It's not too far from where you are now." He recited the address, and she shook Miles as she disconnected.

"Wake up, Miles," she said. "Come on, Blackpaw called and we have a new lead."

"Timmy?"

She caressed his stubbled cheek with her hand. "I don't know for sure, but it's an address for Dugan's mother."

Miles vaulted off the bed and grabbed his clothes and jerked them on.

Hope jumped in Jordan's chest as she dressed, too. Forget the shower. This might lead them to Dugan and Timmy.

MILES RUSHED INTO the bathroom and splashed cold water on his face, not bothering to shower or shave. He hadn't thought he'd sleep at all last night but making love with Jordan had worn him out.

They should probably talk about it, he thought, then dismissed the idea when he stepped into the bedroom and she rushed into the bathroom herself. Minutes later, they grabbed coffee and tortillas from the breakfast buffet in the motel, then jumped in his Jeep.

"You should have let me talk to Blackpaw," Miles said, his tone gruffer than he'd intended.

"You were sleeping so soundly I wanted to let you rest."

"You don't have to take care of me."

"What if I wanted to?" Jordan said with a defiant chin lift.

He fought a tiny smile. He liked her spunky and sassy.

Hell, he liked her any way. Especially naked.

Images of their lovemaking flashed in his mind, but the image of Timmy's bloody T-shirt followed, making him feel guilty as hell for loving her when his son might be hurting.

No...he couldn't think like that.

They lapsed into an awkward quiet as the miles passed and the sun rose to streak the weathered road with rays of morning light. Miles of more desolate land stretched before them. They passed signs leading to several resorts on the gulf, but

left those behind as he turned onto a dirt road that was supposed to lead to farmland.

A truck filled with workers passed, another carrying chickens. Sweat beaded on his skin as he neared the address. He
turned onto another dirt road that led to a dilapidated wooden
house with chickens in the yard and a broken-down rusted
truck parked to the side. Another truck sat half-hidden behind the house, the tail jutting out, revealing a metal storage
bin in the cab.

Miles's blood turned to ice.

Dugan was here. What about his little boy?

"This is it," Jordan said.

Miles parked, drew his gun and ordered her to stay in the
truck.

"Miles, I might be able to help."

"It's too dangerous," he said, "Stay here until I check things
out." Until he found Dugan and killed him.

He didn't want her to witness what he intended to do to
the man.

Chapter Twenty

Miles eased up to the front door and peered inside the window. He spotted a den off a hallway that led to the kitchen. Very little furniture occupied the den, and what was there was ratty and old. A newspaper and coffee cup sat on a tattered coffee table though, indicating someone was in the house.

He peered down the hall and spotted the kitchen sink and stove, then a figure moving. Dugan. He was pacing back and forth waving a knife in his hand.

Anger and adrenaline churned through Miles, and he motioned for Jordan to stay put as he crept around to the back. His boots smothered the weeds, the stench of chickens permeating the air and making it hard to breathe.

Mud stained the glass windowpanes on the side of the house, and he inched closer to the back door. A small window insert offered him a view of Dugan again.

And an old woman who was tied to a wooden kitchen chair.

Dugan paused in front of her, ranting as he jabbed the knife at her in threatening, erratic motions while she trembled in fear. Her skin looked leathery, her face wrinkled and pasty, evidence she'd been a chain-smoker all her life. Patches of stringy gray hair hung down over her shoulders, her eyes sallow and scared.

Miles scanned the room, praying to see Timmy but he

didn't spot him anywhere. Praying his son was in another room, he inched around the house peeking in each window.

But all the rooms were empty.

Rage and grief suffused him, and he made his way to the back door again, then paused to listen. No signs of his son.

Furious, he kicked open the back door. "Put the knife down, Dugan, it's over."

Dugan spun around and waved the knife, his own eyes glazed with a crazy look. Then he reached behind the door and yanked Timmy in front of him.

Miles choked on a breath. Dear God, Timmy was alive.

But Dugan had the knife blade to his throat.

"Daddy?" Timmy whispered, his little chin quivering.

Miles held up a hand. "It's okay, son, I'm here. Just be very still."

Dugan leered at him. "Go away and let me finish what I came to do."

"I know what your mother did to you, but Timmy had nothing to do with it," Miles said, searching his mind for the things Jordan had told him. "Let my little boy go and we'll talk about your mother."

"You're crazy, son, just like I always thought," the old woman said through a smoker's cough. "Good-for-nothing, lying murderer."

"Shut up!" Dugan swirled around, gripping Timmy tighter, then lunged at the woman. "You're the good-for-nothing one, you whore."

"Robert," Jordan said softly.

Miles didn't dare move, but somehow he was grateful she was there behind him. Maybe she could defuse the situation by talking to Dugan.

Although judging from the looks of him, he had delved too deeply into his delusional state for her to break through.

"Robert," she said again in a soothing tone. "We talked

about this before, remember? You don't want to hurt Timmy. He's just a kid like you were back when you wanted someone to rescue you." Jordan eased up beside him, her demeanor so calm that it helped to stem Miles's churning stomach. "You can do that for Timmy now. You can save him and be his hero."

Miles ground his teeth to keep from calling Dugan the murdering bastard he was.

"If you do," Jordan continued in a gentle tone, "I'll let everyone know what you did for him."

"The whores had to die," Dugan shouted, then waved the knife at his mother's face. "They had to die for their sins."

"Just release Timmy," Jordan said. "You aren't angry at him. It's your mother that you're mad at for how she treated you."

Dugan slowly pivoted his head to look at her, then down at Timmy, whose face was pale, his eyes huge in his little face. "Please, mister," Timmy said. "I wanna go home with my daddy."

"See, Timmy has a father that cares about him, that will treat him right," Jordan continued. "I know you wanted that all along, didn't you, Robert? You wanted your daddy to come and rescue you from your mother and what she put you through."

Dugan nodded, a tear slipping down his ruddy cheek. He had once looked polished and smug, but now he looked like a sick, crazed animal caught in a trap.

"Come here, Timmy." Jordan eased closer and held out her hand. "Let him go, Robert, and you can be a savior, like the man you always wanted to save you."

Dugan suddenly released Timmy, and Timmy ran toward Miles, but Dugan grabbed Jordan by the arm. Miles jerked Timmy behind him, then his gaze met Jordan's. She gave a quick nod as if she'd read his mind and knew he was going to shoot.

A second later, Jordan ducked and he fired. The bullet slammed into Dugan's chest. He looked shocked for a moment, then his hand flew to his chest where blood pooled, and he staggered back against the kitchen sink.

Jordan jerked away and raced toward him. Miles caught her, and she grabbed Timmy and cradled him against her, pulling him back toward the opened door.

The old woman muttered a string of profanity, berating Dugan and spilling hatred for her own son. "Got what you deserved," she said, then broke into another terrible cough.

Dugan suddenly lunged toward Miles, but Miles fired another round, and Dugan slumped to the floor with an anguished cry at his mother's feet.

She shoved his body away with her foot, and Dugan rolled over and looked up at her, blood seeping from his chest. "It was your fault," he choked out. "All those women... I wanted to kill you instead."

"Go to hell," the old woman muttered. Then she turned her head toward Miles. "Untie me now."

Miles glared at her, the disturbing inclination to let her rot for what she'd done to her son eating at him. She had started the chain of events that had led to so many senseless deaths, to Dugan's sickness.

And to the fact that Miles had almost lost his son.

But he was a man of the law, and he knew he had to do the right thing. His son was watching, and he'd seen enough violence and evil in his lifetime. Miles wanted to be a man he would be proud of.

Then his son whispered his name, and Miles knew he had a second chance.

He would never let Timmy down again.

Five days later

JORDAN WATCHED THE special awards ceremony where the boys' achievements over the past two weeks were acknowledged with a mixture of joy and sadness. Carlos, Justin, Wayling, Malcolm and Rory all received awards for bravery, and Timmy was awarded a special certificate for toughest cowboy on the horizon.

Two days ago, the press had run a story, complete with photographs of her, the kids and Miles, detailing the events that had led to Ables's arrest and Dugan's death. Miles had been the true hero though and was receiving a commendation from the governor for finally solving the Slasher case. Janet Bridges had also come forward and admitted that Dugan had hidden his dark side from her; she had found trophies of the victims, but run out of fear for her life.

Ables had been born when Dugan was a teen and the old woman had given him away, but he'd come looking for his family and thought he might find it with his brother.

Pride filled Jordan as Timmy stood up to speak in front of all the other kids. He had made tremendous strides in his progress since they had returned to the BBL. The nurturing hands of the workers, the other boys who talked more openly about their own struggles and Miles's constant attention had turned him back into a happy child once again.

Not that he didn't still grieve for his mother, but Jordan had helped him realize that talking about her was okay, that missing her was okay, that his mother would want him to be happy though, and that she was always with him.

She walked to her cabin, her heart aching. She had fallen hopelessly in love with Miles, but since their return, they hadn't shared a private moment. Hadn't talked about the night they'd made love.

In fact, an awkward chasm had fallen between them.

Miles didn't love her. Like Marie said, he was married to his job.

And she couldn't keep him from what he wanted.

She had given herself to him out of love and comfort, not because she expected anything in return.

Miles had enough on his plate being a single father. And one day soon, she was sure, he would return to his job. He was too good at it not to. She'd also heard he'd been hunting for a small ranch to buy himself.

Then he and Timmy would have a home and be gone from her life forever.

Tears blurred her eyes at the thought, and she turned to leave. Timmy suddenly ran toward her then thrust a piece of paper in her hand. Miles strolled up behind him, his hands in his pockets, a sheepish look on his face.

"What's this?" she asked.

"It's what I see when I close my eyes now. No more red."

She smiled and patted his shoulder, then studied the picture. It was his drawing of her and Miles and him, the three of them hand in hand. Stars glittered brightly from the night sky shining a halo around them.

Her heart squeezed.

"Those two stars are touching," she said as she noticed two of the brightest ones in the corner, their points coinciding.

"You told me Mommy lived in heaven. That's her." Timmy pointed to the bigger star. "And that's your little brother. Mommy tolded me she'd take care of him till you got to heaven, since you took care of me."

Jordan's heart thumped wildly, and she looked up at Miles. His expression looked as stunned as hers.

"Did you tell him?" she asked.

Miles shook his head no.

"I told you," Timmy said. "Mommy did." He tugged her arm down and gave her a big sloppy kiss. "She likes you."

Then he turned and ran back to the other boys. Jordan saw the shock on Miles's face, and her stomach tumbled to her throat. She wanted to believe that the three of them could be together, but Miles had made no declaration of love. It was only Timmy's childish wishful thinking.

Unable to speak for the emotions clogging her throat, she gave him a slight wave, then turned and ran toward her cabin.

Images of her little brother hit her, then images of Timmy and Miles, and tears spilled over. She was glad she was alone and in the dark so no one could see them.

A chill had set in, and she swiped at her wet cheeks, then rubbed her arms, tugged her key from her pocket and let herself into her cabin.

She thought she'd left a light on, but the room was bathed in darkness. Then a sound squeaked. A footstep.

Jordan froze, her senses alert. Dugan was dead... Had Ables escaped?

Her derringer was locked in the desk drawer and she headed toward it, but suddenly someone grabbed her from behind and put her in a strangling choke hold.

MILES WATCHED JORDAN disappear with a dull throbbing in his chest. He had been so relieved to have Timmy back alive and so worried about his health that he hadn't had time to think about what had happened between him and Jordan.

He'd assumed that the sex had been a frantic, emotionally charged release of pent-up frustration at the time.

But deep down he knew it was more.

He simply hadn't been ready to face it or the questions that the possibility of an ongoing relationship with Jordan brought.

The complications...his job...her feelings...his...Timmy's...

Hell, he didn't want to *think* about it. He just knew what he wanted.

He wanted Jordan.

In his life. In his bed.

With him and his son.

For good.

Determination suddenly cleared his head of the questions and doubts. Timmy's drawing and comment about Marie had also dissipated his guilt.

Jordan had helped his son see that he could still love his mother while he moved on. That it was okay for him to love Jordan.

Just as it was okay for him to love her.

But he'd seen the emotions on her face when Timmy had given her the drawing of the three of them—did she not want them in her future?

Would she feel the same as Marie—that he was married to his job?

Dammit. He had to know.

He laid his hand on his little boy's shoulder. "You okay, son?"

Timmy nodded. "Can I spend the night with the other campers tonight?"

Miles barely breathed, he was so happy. He and Carlos had discussed this earlier, but he hadn't been sure Timmy was ready.

It was such a monumental step that he wanted to jump for joy and shout his thanks above.

But he stooped and gave Timmy a knuckle-up instead. "Sure, son. Have fun."

Timmy threw his arms around him and hugged him, then ran back to the group. Miles gestured to Carlos to watch out for him, and Carlos nodded that he would.

A sense of relief filled Miles and lightened his mood, and he strode toward Jordan's cabin. Now that he knew what he wanted, he couldn't wait to tell her.

The nerves he expected left him, and he practically jogged to her cabin. As he neared it though, he noticed a light burning in the den, then saw the silhouette of two bodies through the window.

Two bodies?

He froze, wondering if Jordan might have company. A friend? Lover?

No...

Then he spotted movement, the silhouette of a hand holding a knife, and his instincts kicked in. Automatically he reached for his gun and slipped up the steps to the porch, crept to the edge of the window, pausing to listen.

"Please, you don't want to do this," Jordan pleaded.

"Didn't think we'd see your picture in the paper, you stupid bitch."

The voice, low and throaty, trying to sound adult. A teenager.

The memory of Jordan's brother's death and her fear of gang retaliation struck him, and he realized the publicity over Dugan's arrest had placed her in the limelight.

And brought danger to her door.

Dammit, he had just found her. Had just realized how much he loved her.

He and Timmy couldn't lose her now. She was their future, their life.

Chapter Twenty-One

Miles inched up to the door, eased it open and crept inside, careful to make his footsteps light. Still, his boots must have hit a weak spot in the floor because the plank squeaked and the big guy holding Jordan swung around, the knife at her throat.

Déjà vu of Dugan's attack on Jordan hit him, nearly blinding him, but Jordan's voice broke through the haze. "Please, there's no reason to do this. What you did to my brother is over, but I can help you if you let me."

Dear Lord. Jordan was trying to help the kid who had her in his clutches.

She was a fool.

And the most courageous, wonderful woman he'd ever met.

But he didn't give a damn about the kid. Not if he hurt Jordan.

He raised his gun and pointed it at the teenager. "Listen, I'm a cop and a damn good shot. And I've taken down a lot bigger, tougher men than you."

The kid was big, angry and, judging from his tattoos, a member of the gang who had killed Jordan's brother. Here to get retribution for her testimony against one of his own.

Loyalty misplaced.

Angry lines slashed grooves around the boy's face, accentuating the scar on his jaw. A knife wound. Probably a gang fight.

"Let her go, man. I'm a lawman. There's no way this is going to have a happy ending."

"Please," Jordan said gently. "There are people who can help you. I'll help you."

The kid released a curse. "Why the hell would you help me, lady?"

"Because you're young, and you've had a tough life, but I think you can do better." Jordan gripped his hand where he had it at her throat. "My brother wouldn't want anyone else to die."

Miles kept his gun trained on the teen. "Do as she says and no one gets hurt."

The kid looked him in the eye, and for a moment, Miles thought he was going to fight. But he dropped the knife to the floor instead and released Jordan. Miles vaulted forward, spun the kid around and handcuffed him.

"Miles—"

He cut her off. "He'll have his day in court, but I can't let him go. Not with all the other boys' lives at stake."

Her eyes glittered with emotions, but she knew he was right. Then he called the sheriff's number. Jordan continued to talk to the kid and encourage him to seek help while they waited on him to arrive.

Miles had no idea if the teenager had any redeemable qualities, but his admiration and love for Jordan grew because he knew she wouldn't give up.

As soon as the sheriff left with the boy, he planned to tell her how he felt.

JORDAN'S HEART TUGGED with sadness as the teenager was arrested. She hoped he'd let her help him, but she also realized she couldn't save everyone.

Timmy's drawing caught her attention where it lay on the

table and she smiled. His childlike insight and wisdom brought tears to her eyes.

Miles stepped back inside, then gave her a fierce look and gripped her arms with his hands. "God, Jordan, I was scared when I saw he had you."

Jordan's heart stuttered. She had been afraid, too. "Why did you come here, Miles? Did you know he was here?"

He shook his head, a flicker of possessiveness back in his eyes. "No, I came to tell you that I love you."

Her mouth curved into a surprised smile. "You do?"

He nodded. "The past few days I was so worried about Timmy, and trying to figure out what to do, where we would go. I felt so guilty over Marie—"

"You can't keep blaming yourself," Jordan said quietly. "She wouldn't want that. And Timmy needs you to forgive yourself."

"I'm working on it." His jaw tightened, then relaxed a fraction of a second later as if he was trying to do just that. "I've been looking for land, and I bought a small spread."

"I heard you were looking," Jordan said softly. "That you were leaving..."

"I am, but the ranch is close by. I want to be a part of the BBL and I want Timmy to be part of it, too." Hunger deepened his expression. "But I want you to come with us." He nuzzled her neck. "I want you to marry me, Jordan."

Jordan's heart soared with happiness.

Then he lifted her chin and forced her to look at him. "Jordan?"

"I love you, too, Miles." She licked her suddenly dry lips.

"I can't promise I'll leave the job, but we can talk about it," he murmured.

"No, you're good at what you do. It's who you are. I would never ask you to give up your work." She pressed a kiss to his jaw. "The world needs men like you. Men who fight for justice and teach kids how to overcome obstacles and do what's right."

A tenderness flickered onto his face as if her words had touched a chord deep inside him. But uncertainty lingered there as well. "Then you will be my wife?"

Jordan threaded her fingers in his hair. "Yes, Miles. I love you and I'll marry you."

She kissed him with all her heart, then he took her to bed, and they made love long into the night, sealing their whispered promises of loving with erotic touches that would forever stay in her mind.

And when Jordan stirred and looked through the window at the stars twinkling in the sky, she saw two of the brightest stars she'd ever seen.

Just like Timmy's drawing, their points were touching as if Marie and her brother were holding hands, shining their approval down on the BBL.

And on her and Miles and Timmy and the love that they shared, and the family that they would be together.

* * * * *

Award-winning author Rita Herron's
BUCKING BRONC LODGE *miniseries*
continues next month with NATIVE COWBOY.
Look for it wherever
Harlequin Intrigue books are sold!

COMING NEXT MONTH from Harlequin® Intrigue®
AVAILABLE JANUARY 2, 2013

#1395 STANDOFF AT MUSTANG RIDGE
Delores Fossen

After a one-night stand with bad boy Deputy Royce McCall, Texas heiress Sophie Conway might be pregnant with Royce's baby. And the possible pregnancy has unleashed a killer.

#1396 NATIVE COWBOY
Bucking Bronc Lodge
Rita Herron

When a selfless pregnant doctor becomes the target of a ruthless serial killer, she has no choice but to turn to the man who walked away from her months ago...the father of her child.

#1397 SOLDIER'S REDEMPTION
The Legacy
Alice Sharpe

Cole Bennett is at an impossible impasse: seek the truth of his past, though it threatens to destroy any chance of a future with the woman he loves, or turn away....

#1398 ALPHA ONE
Shadow Agents
Cynthia Eden

If Juliana James wants to stay alive, then she must trust navy SEAL Logan Quinn. But trusting Logan isn't easy...he's the man who broke her heart ten years before.

#1399 INTERNAL AFFAIRS
Alana Matthews

When Sheriff's Deputy Rafe Franco answers a callout on a domestic dispute, he has no idea that he's about to step into his past...and into the arms of the woman he had once loved.

#1400 BRIDAL FALLS RANCH RANSOM
Jan Hambright

Eve Brooks's beautiful face was erased by an explosion alongside a dark highway. But with former FBI agent J. P. Ryker's help, can she discover her inner beauty and strength before her tormenter strikes again?

You can find more information on upcoming Harlequin® titles, free excerpts and more at www.Harlequin.com.

HICNM1212

REQUEST YOUR FREE BOOKS!
2 FREE NOVELS PLUS 2 FREE GIFTS!

Harlequin
INTRIGUE
BREATHTAKING ROMANTIC SUSPENSE

YES! Please send me 2 FREE Harlequin Intrigue® novels and my 2 FREE gifts (gifts are worth about $10). After receiving them, if I don't wish to receive any more books, I can return the shipping statement marked "cancel." If I don't cancel, I will receive 6 brand-new novels every month and be billed just $4.49 per book in the U.S. or $5.24 per book in Canada. That's a saving of at least 14% off the cover price! It's quite a bargain! Shipping and handling is just 50¢ per book in the U.S. and 75¢ per book in Canada.* I understand that accepting the 2 free books and gifts places me under no obligation to buy anything. I can always return a shipment and cancel at any time. Even if I never buy another book, the two free books and gifts are mine to keep forever.

182/382 HDN FEQ2

Name _____ (PLEASE PRINT) _____

Address _____ Apt. # _____

City _____ State/Prov. _____ Zip/Postal Code _____

Signature (if under 18, a parent or guardian must sign) _____

Mail to the **Reader Service:**
IN U.S.A.: P.O. Box 1867, Buffalo, NY 14240-1867
IN CANADA: P.O. Box 609, Fort Erie, Ontario L2A 5X3
Not valid for current subscribers to Harlequin Intrigue books.

**Are you a subscriber to Harlequin Intrigue books
and want to receive the larger-print edition?
Call 1-800-873-8635 or visit www.ReaderService.com.**

* Terms and prices subject to change without notice. Prices do not include applicable taxes. Sales tax applicable in N.Y. Canadian residents will be charged applicable taxes. Offer not valid in Quebec. This offer is limited to one order per household. All orders subject to credit approval. Credit or debit balances in a customer's account(s) may be offset by any other outstanding balance owed by or to the customer. Please allow 4 to 6 weeks for delivery. Offer available while quantities last.

Your Privacy—The Reader Service is committed to protecting your privacy. Our Privacy Policy is available online at www.ReaderService.com or upon request from the Reader Service.

We make a portion of our mailing list available to reputable third parties that offer products we believe may interest you. If you prefer that we not exchange your name with third parties, or if you wish to clarify or modify your communication preferences, please visit us at www.ReaderService.com/consumerschoice or write to us at Reader Service Preference Service, P.O. Box 9062, Buffalo, NY 14269. Include your complete name and address.

HI11B